ZANDROS
in Love

JEANE MOORE

CALUMET EDITIONS

Minneapolis

SECOND EDITION DECEMBER 2022

This is a work of fiction. Names, characters, places
and incidents either are the product of the author's imagination
or are used fictitiously.

ISBN – 978-1-960250-29-2

10 9 8 7 6 5 4 3 2
Cover art and book design by Gary Lindberg

ZANDROS
in Love

JEANE MOORE

CALUMET EDITIONS

Minneapolis

2009
SUNDAY, NOVEMBER 22

S he never went away. She was there, in my thoughts, maybe just a wisp of her lurking in the back of my mind, but always there. Sometimes it almost made me angry, like now, sitting down to a big-money game. I pushed her away and focused on the cards I had just picked up.

Seven-deuce off suit. Christ. Not what I could call an auspicious start. Good thing I wasn't superstitious.

I had a simple goal: strike fear into the hearts and guts of a bunch of Hollywood poseurs. I was there to be Weiss's poker-table bully boy. That's not what he said when he invited me, but that was what he expected. What he wanted. Counted on. Ex street brawler.

High-stakes, by invitation only. An expensive room in an expensive house, a Beverly Hills faux half-timbered California Tudor manor house. Eight of us, all in evening black, because the host liked it that way, sitting in padded leather armchairs around a felt-covered table decorated with stacks of colored chips. Male opulence, Hollywood division. I knew the others only slightly. I'd played with most of them before, but we'd never socialized outside of that room. I was not in their league away from the table. And at least some of them were wondering what the hell I was doing there.

Our host, Weiss, produced movies. Their titles: *High Concept* and *Blockbuster*. Weiss's middle names? *Money* and *Power*. He had both in spades, and he liked using them.

As we gathered, Weiss, in the number one chair, said, "Get another drink, Brooks. I don't want you getting up for more after we start playing." Brooks obediently got up from the number two chair and went to the bar.

Brooks played with his wife's and two ex-wives' money. Probably some of the others played with family money too, like Brooks and I did. But by and large, when I played poker, I took money out of their families and into mine.

The guy next to me, chair number three, was Sullivan, a squash-faced old Irishman who had once been a boxer and then a television comic. At the table he was an ATM. Without any urging, old Sully was also up and at the bar.

Weiss said, "Zandros? Top you up?"

I said, "I'm good, thanks."

A courtesy to the outsider. They were all cronies and underlings of Weiss and older than I was by a couple of decades at least. Except for Miller. Miller was close to my age and not connected to the industry, as they call it. The industry.

Miller's drink of choice? Fizzy water. He bore watching.

Me, Poller, Miller, and Gooding. Four, five, six, and seven.

A total stranger played in chair number eight getting some sideways glances from the other players. A broad-set muscular man, medium height, with a wide muscular pale face and flat dark hair and flat dark eyes. Mid-forties. Weiss introduced him: Hugh Black. He had an outrider, a tall thin fair-haired guy with excellent posture who sat near the door and watched quietly. No one introduced him but when we stopped for drinks I heard Black call him Carl.

Weiss always used a pro dealer. Dante. Very good. Knew his business. He'd only dealt to me twice before, but tonight he greeted me by name before he started his patter. Weiss introduced him around and I heard Sullivan mutter "Fucking Mex fags". I watched Dante wash the deck and shuffle. Beautiful hands. Well shaped, well cared for. Nails manicured, cut short, shaped, no polish. Not a queen, just a man with his share of pride. I wondered if he thought all of us were assholes under the suits.

Dante said, "Good evening, gentlemen. Tonight's game is no-limit Texas hold 'em. Blinds are 25 and 50. The game is table stakes, and the usual house rules apply."

He dealt the first hand.

I pretended to sip at the lowball glass half full of Cognac, wetting my upper lip and then licking it, savoring the taste. Weiss served good liquor. Maybe when this was over I would drink some.

I looked at my cards. Seven-deuce off suit. Christ.

Later I told myself I should have gone back to the hotel right then. At the table I was barely in the game. Couldn't do anything except get out-drawn or fail to make some good starters better. After blowing through my first buy-in I re-bought for another 50K, and dropped almost half of that. Sullivan was grinning at me. Was the bully boy an empty threat?

Brooks said, "Somebody's baby ain't gettin' her new shoes."

Did they smell blood in the water?

I never talked at the table. I heard only what I needed to hear and said only what I needed to say. I heard that. *Malaka.* I laughed and looked at my cards again. Ace of hearts, jack of diamonds. Tossing in two green chips, I said, "I'll call the fifty."

Poller says, "To me? I'm in." He sounded surprised.

Black spoke for almost the first time. "You seem distracted, Mr. Zandros."

Sullivan said, "Mus' be pussy."

Miller: "Raise. Play for two hundred."

Miller was the one to watch out for, all right. He had a face that reminded me of Harry and he made his money in software engineering. He started the company at the right time, then he owned the company, then he sold the company at the right time. Now he played high-stakes poker.

Sullivan announced, like we didn't know, "*Some*body likes his hand."

Miller looked mildly interested. "You folding?"

Dante jumped in fast. "The action is still over here, gentlemen," and he gently patted the table in front of Gooding. "It's on you, sir." Gooding folded.

Black said, "Maybe you'd like to tell us about her. Get it off your chest."

Brooks snickered.

Black said, "I've heard that confession is good for the soul."

This was weird. He didn't seem like the chatty type.

I said, "Soul's okay, but thanks for the offer." *Was* I okay? Was I in fact being distracted by those buzzing thoughts of Clare that never quite went away? Brush him off. "When I win this game, maybe I'll tell you about her."

And maybe I won't. I didn't want to talk about her.

Certainly not about the first time I saw her: She came into Vincent's Bar out of a February snowstorm, right toward me but then I realized it was toward Harry, who was standing next to me. He draped a casual arm over her shoulders and I felt a stab of jealousy in my gut that damn near took me to my knees. She had dark dark hair, all soft curls, and fair smooth skin, like fine new paper, and a straight nose reddened by the cold, and those incredible, impossible blue eyes. Large. Deep blue. Eyes that knew everything about me, that I could swim away in and never need to come back. I wanted her to close them so no one else would see them. I realized Harry had just said, "Careful."

That was in February, and still she buzzed.

Black said, "*When*? Not *if*?"

I grinned at him. "It's always *when*, not *if*."

Weiss, who was the small blind that hand, called the two hundred, Brooks and Sullivan both tossed their cards, and Miller said to me, "Zandros." Like he was tasting my name.

"Yeah." I put in two black chips and took back my two green chips to call.

Dante pulled all the bets into the pot, rapped the table twice, slid the corner of the top card under the chips, counted off three cards, and fanned them face up in front of him, evenly spaced and perfectly aligned.

A jack, a ten, and a seven.

Weiss said, "I loves me a good rainbow flop. Three hundred," and set out three black chips.

Miller said, "Zandros? You in?"

Top pair, top kicker. I considered it for a moment, said, "Seven hundred," and put out seven black chips.

Weiss said, "And I'm out," and tossed his cards.

Dante mucked Weiss's cards, then turned to Weiss and said firmly, "Act in turn, please. The action is on Mr. Miller."

Weiss mumbled, "Sorry. Didn't see his cards," even though Miller's cards were in plain sight of everybody at the table.

Miller looked at me, smiled, and said, "This could get interesting. I hear Turks got leather balls. Make it two thousand all day," and tossed out two yellow chips.

I smiled for him. "Greeks." Does he really have eight, nine? I looked at him across the table, like my interest was entirely academic. "Call."

Dante pulled in the bets and put up the turn. An ace.

Top two pair now. Let's see if he's got the straight or if he's on a draw. I threw out five yellow chips.

"Five thousand to call, Mr. Miller," Dante said.

"Make it ten," Miller said, putting out his bet.

What the fuck? "Call."

Dante put up the river and it's another jack. Sullivan said, "Jack, ten, seven, ace, jack. Who's got the boat?"

Dante said, "Mr. Sullivan! Do not be commenting on the board or calling out possible hands while there's still action going on. Is that clear?"

Sullivan said, "Hey, who the hell you think you are?"

Weiss said, "He's the dealer. Behave or leave, your choice."

"Okay, okay." Sullivan turned to Dante and tossed him a green chip.

Dante picked up the chip, tapped it twice on the edge of the chip tray, put it with the other tips in his fanny pack, and said, "Thank you, sir." Turning to face me, he said, "Action's on you, Mr. Zandros."

I hesitated.

"Mr. Zandros? Check or bet, please." I hesitated again.

Miller said, "Whatcha gonna do, Sam?" Not impatient but maybe a little amused.

Was I so open? I really did hope so. "Check."

Miller leaned back in his chair and looked at me. "All in."

Ah. Hooked. Reel him in. I said, "Call."

Miller turned up his hand and showed his ace seven. He'd missed the full house. But his expression didn't change. Not by an atom.

I showed my hand and tossed my cards in. Dante counted Miller's chips, then mine. Final score Miller $31,275, Zandros $31,250. Dante took one green chip from Miller's stack, gently set it in front of him, and pushed the rest to me.

Weiss said, "You want a re-buy, Miller?"

Miller said, "Sure." Jesus he was cool.

Suddenly *when not if* went to work in my blood. The cards started running hot and I could do no wrong. Three more hours, I had all of Brooks's money, all of Gooding's, all of Sullivan's, and a big chunk of Poller's. And maybe Weiss's pocket change. He probably had barrels of the stuff in his faux Tudor dungeons. Maybe it was faux money.

Miller'd gotten both his buy-ins back and then some from Weiss, Poller, and Black. A big pile of Black's. It looked like Miller and I had come out about even.

The natives were getting restless. Poller and Gooding left, looking unhappy, but not so much that they might irritate Weiss. They thanked him for his hospitality. Always a pleasure. Sullivan wandered off with a drink in his hand and in a minute we could hear a TV pitchman selling a combination juicer-blender-coffee grinder. Weiss called a stop and cashed out the rest of us.

I drank off my glass of Cognac and stood up. "I'll see you gentlemen another time?" The prospect didn't seem to cheer them up. Sliding a half dozen yellow chips over to him, I said, "Dante, you deal a great game."

Brooks locked in on those yellow chips and I wondered if he was going to grab them and run.

I picked up the locking metal briefcase containing the ten grand that I knew better than to risk tonight, added the bundles of cash I had just acquired, shook hands with Weiss, made eye contact with Miller for a second and nodded, and headed for my car.

Monday, November 23

1

Black's voice was behind me. "Mr. Zandros."

I stopped and turned. "Mr. Black."

"I'd like to have a drink with you, and some conversation."

I considered. I was coming down from an adrenaline high. I could use a drink and some talk and maybe a blondie. Why not?

I said, "Sure."

"Where are you staying?"

"The Chequers. There's a bar across the street that'll be open."

He said, "Carl will find it. We'll meet you in the bar. Twenty minutes."

The early morning overcast was thinning and brightening when I parked by my hotel. I had just enough time to put all my cash into the safe in my room and jog across the street and see them walk into the bar ahead of me. I knew Carl had seen me coming. I entered and stepped to one side to stand with my back to the wall while I let my eyes adjust. A habit I'd learned from Harry a long time ago.

The bar wasn't crowded at this hour. A guy with the shakes and another one who looked too gray to stand upright were sitting at the bar. Two girlies at a table near the door. Black had taken a round table in the back, by the wall. Carl was still standing, to gently urge me into a chair next to Black. Then he seated himself on my other side. A barman in a still-clean apron came out to take our order. Black ordered a Hennessy XO and Carl got fizzy water. I ordered a double Balvenie.

Black said, "You're a scotch drinker."

I said, "I am."

"But at Weiss's you were pretending to drink brandy."

I didn't answer.

He said, "I'm glad I got a chance to see you really play back there. It's almost… mesmerizing at times."

I laughed. "Now you see it, now you don't."

"That was a hell of a bluff you ran on Miller. I was surprised he went for it."

I said, "He didn't."

He said, "But he…" He stopped.

I said, "You went for it." So did the others but they didn't count.

"You and Miller set it up?"

"Nope. But we both knew an opportunity when we saw one. We've both seen it done before. Done it ourselves. How much did you discount him as a player after that?"

The drinks came and I took a small sip to prepare my mouth, then a bigger one.

Black smoldered for a minute, then let it go. He said, "You promised to tell me about what our friend Sully so gallantly called *pussy*."

"Did I promise? I believe I said maybe."

"Maybe you did." He smiled with his mouth. "Something was distracting you, and I wanted to know what would break your concentration in such an important game. I'm interested in what people here call the backstory of a game in which I lost, if not a bundle, at least a roll."

I leaned back, sipped some more. Sucked a bigger swallow into my mouth and chewed it thoughtfully. Do him a favor or not? I said, "You have a tell."

I felt Carl lean forward.

Black said, "I do?"

"Yes."

Pause.

He said a bit testily, "You can't stop now."

"If you have good hole cards, you hold them in your hand. If not, you leave them on the table."

"That's it?"

"It's enough." I felt Carl lean back.

He looked miffed. Then his expression smoothed out. Next time we played, that tell would be gone.

I said, "My backstory is a woman named Clare. She's a photographer, and none of your business. Stay away from her."

Carl didn't move.

Black said, "She's not in the cards. I was curious about... what she means to you. And now I know." He finished his Cognac and Carl picked up the glass and went to the bar.

Black leaned back. He said, "The Zandros brothers. Born Alexandros. Paul plays the horses, badly, and poker, badly. Philip and two uncles run the betting operation. Sam and Andy play high-stakes poker. Andy's very good, and if you aren't already the best player between Atlantic City and Vegas, you could be. You've been playing mid-level players in mid-level games, but not in the top levels. You need a challenge. I want to invest in that."

"How?"

"Staking you in some games. I can put up more than you and your brothers can, and I can set you up with some very big players. You win more even after I take my cut."

"Which is?"

"Standard. I recover my buy-in and take fifty percent of what's left."

"And if I lose?"

He shrugged. "I take the loss. I'm a reasonable man."

"That's not standard. Most backers want the buy-in back, no matter what. What else?"

"That's all. The Zandros brothers can go on as before. You can play as much as you want, just so I get the games when and where *I* want."

"Where?"

"Chicago, Kansas City, Louisville. Houston, Denver. Vegas. Wherever the money is. There's a lot of money out there. You just have to go get it."

I didn't say anything.

He said, "I suggest you think it over." Now he did smile. "I think you like being the street brawler with a master's degree. The scar on your face is a badge of honor. No plastic surgery or Hollywood makeup job. It's intimidating but it also says no B.S."

The scar on my face was almost invisible these days. It was the outcome of a meeting with a very sharp knife in the hands of another sixteen-year-old over, of course, a girl. Diagonally across my forehead, skip over the eye socket, down the cheek to the jaw bone. Badge of honor. Who *was* this guy?

I said, "I'm not looking for a job offer."

He said, "Like I said, think about it."

I swallowed the rest of the scotch and stood. We all stood. "Time to sleep," I said. "Very interesting to meet you." I smiled and shook hands (Carl stepped back to adroitly and almost unnoticeably avoid the handshake), and I left.

2

In my hotel room, instead of sleeping, and instead of a blondie, I lay on the bed sipping whisky and ran the film of the game. When it came to cards, I had my own private little cinema.

As soon as my big brother Philip let me and Andy hold the deck of pretty pictures—we were four and he was fourteen—and started to teach us their names, he realized that we had something special in memorization skills. He didn't tell anyone but read up on it himself and found that it was called an *eidetic* memory. Sometimes called a *photographic* memory. He told us that it was a secret. Exciting as hell, a secret with Philip.

He taught us cards. In time he taught us to go back over every game, remember every card played, analyze every hand, and we still did it, he and Andy and I, every game we played. Together if we were in the same game, alone if not. I didn't know, or care, what Paul did. From long practice Philip was very very good. Andy was close to perfect, but maybe not quite. He never cared as much. I was perfect.

So. Last night. Cast and crew. Weiss. A box-shaped head on a barrel-shaped body. Not there for the game or the money. There to own the other players.

Waspy Brooks, who I had seen splashing the pot three times. I knew Weiss had seen it too, and now he owned Brooks if he didn't already.

Sullivan, who looked like he'd dressed out of a laundry bag.

Me. A moviegoer at my own memory, I see myself. Thirty-two years old. Dark hair, dark eyes, a little over medium tall—five-eleven in socks. Long legs. Lean, not skinny. In shape. Perfectly at ease in dinner jacket in the expensive room in the expensive house. Like I'd never even seen fucking Rice Street.

Poller. Forgettable. Take a little, lose a little. Probably down ten bucks for the whole evening. A spectator.

Miller. *Damn* him. Best I'd played with for a long time. Almost as good as Harry. Almost as good as goddamn Andy. And that sharp eye and slightly mocking voice, trying to catch me out, make me mad. He never did but he came close.

Gooding. Another nonentity. Wouldn't know him on the street.

Black. What did he really want? Money, of course. Backstory? Bullshit. Money. Why was he interested in Clare? Clare didn't have any money. But I did and she had me.

Who was he? Everything said mob. Ask Uncle Cy.

I ran it again. And again. Looked at every card in every hand. Looked at every move, listened to every voice.

After some hours of that, and some dozing and waking and dozing and waking, I got up, said, "Fuck it," and headed for the shower. I wanted nothing more than to hit someone, and I suspected that getting into the ring at the gym would not do the trick. Fucking monkey brain. I dressed and packed up my duffle, checked out, and went home. To St. Paul.

TUESDAY, NOVEMBER 24

We had two rooms in an elderly commercial building in Lowertown, the old part of downtown St. Paul, where we ran our family business. Making book. We were bookies.

Our office, unlabeled and unnamed, had large windows that actually opened, lots of woodwork, dark wood wainscoting, high ceilings, uneven wooden floors, and incandescent ceiling lights that didn't light much. I had always liked being there.

In the inner room, there were three old wooden desks, with big old wooden swivel chairs. The desks each held a laptop computer and piles of paper and reading lamps and cheap cell phones. There was a conference table and several plain wooden chairs. There was also a large, worn, upholstered armchair, and a big flat-screen TV and three satellite TVs in one corner. It was Uncle Nick's self-appointed job to watch the TV sports channels, games and commentators, for as many hours a day as he could stand it.

Everyone was there that Tuesday morning—Uncle Nick, Uncle Cy, Philip, Paul, Andy, me.

Except for Uncle Cy we gathered in the inner room. Andy started coffee, and Uncle Nick sat down in his easy chair and fired up the big flat-screen TV to the first ESPN show of his daily schedule, getting the audio through a set of headphones. He had the three smaller satellite TV sets hooked to a switchbox that Andy'd set up and he flipped back and forth between sets and channels and we kidded him about getting his own show on CNN. This week it was all football. Thanksgiving Day was one of the biggest betting days of the year, and he'd be on the TVs and the phones all day today and tomorrow and into Thursday until we locked down at the first kickoff.

Paul combed his hair and checked his shave in the small mirror he had hung in the corner. He had on yet another of his ugly, trendy suits that looked like it came from Discount Menswear. It didn't. He paid big bucks but he looked like *he* came from Discount Menswear.

Philip powered up the number one computer and watched spread-sheets open while he took off his suit jacket and vest—blue-gray wool blend—and put them on his special hangar on the hook on the wall. Crisp white-on-white shirt and gray suspenders and tie. His brokerage look.

Uncle Nick wore a gray suit. He always wore a gray suit. Andy and I wondered how many he owned. They all fit him very well and were made of good cloth but they were all gray.

And if we could see around the corner, we would see Uncle Cy in a dark blue suit with a sweater vest and white shirt under it. Very classic.

In Southern California one dresses up a bit so I'd dressed up a bit while I was there. But that got old fast. Today I gave thanks and wore my usual office comfort look: hoodie, T-shirt, and levis; Andy was in levis and cashmere pullover. We had no dress code, although Philip had once threatened us with one when Andy showed up from an all-night gig looking like he'd fallen into a ravine. He never explained it.

I opened up the number two computer and started looking at sports scores. Andy had number three going and started the day's never-ending data entry and number crunching.

In the outer room Cy opened the vault and got all his computers and surveillance cameras going. He also controlled all three back-room computers whenever he wanted to. He was our tech and money genius.

Still watching his screens, Philip uncovered a plate of pastries that Sofia had sent—little cream-cheese-filled fried pies called myzithropitas.

"Bless her," I said. "I'm madly in love with your wife, Philip."

"You're madly in love with her myzithropitas," he said calmly.

"That, too."

My family wasn't huge, but the extent to which everyone looked like everyone else and the amount of noise they could make and the amount of pressure they could exert and the amount of love everyone (well, almost everyone) lavished on everyone else (almost everyone else) always made them seem like a crowd.

Closest to me in family terms were my two brothers and my sister. The oldest was Paul, then Philip, then Catherine. I was the baby. Catherine was next, eight years older. Philip was a ten-years-older version of me. Paul was a twelve-years-older, heavier, coarser, drunker bad example.

Closest to me in age—in more than age—but in what? Spirit? Soul? Love? All of those. My cousin Andy, just three weeks younger, raised with me because his parents died when we were six. We looked, as my father used to say, like "two Greeks in a pod", and we didn't march in lockstep but it'd be hard to think of how we could have been closer.

We moved from the desks to sit around the conference table next to the big bay window. There had been reports from L.A. all along, me to them, so all I had to talk about was my last night. Telling them the game was easy and I was honest. Honesty had always been an iron-clad family rule.

Then I told them about Black.

None of them spoke. Finally Uncle Nick said, "I don't like that kind of attention."

Philip said, "None of us do." He raised his voice. "Cy. Will you join us for a minute?"

He came quietly in. He always moved very quietly. He had taught Andy and me how to use knives and how to use fighting sticks and a few other fighting moves. But he never talked about how he knew such things. We only knew it had happened in Vietnam or near there. He fascinated us and we watched and listened closely for clues.

Philip said, "Tell Cy about Black.

I repeated all of it. Everyone listened, even, wonder of wonders, Paul.

Philip repeated what Uncle Nick had said: "We don't want that kind of attention."

Paul came out of his chair flinging his arms wide. "Well, you're wrong. Jesus H. *Christ* you're wrong. You're all wrong. Bunch of pussies, all of you." He stalked around to the front of the table. "Family fucking business. Don't catch anyone's attention. Dole out the shares no matter who brings the money *in*. Fucking college boys ain't *they* cute. You dumb fucks, we *need* that kind of attention. That looks to me like big money. Why say no? I say get 'm in here. Call 'm up. Hey Mr. Black let's do some business. Can't you figure it out? We're talking *cash*. Bunch of old men and women and pussies running this *family* business."

I said to Paul, "Like *you're* bringing in the money? You haven't had more than one month out of ten in the black since Nick Dandolos died."

Andy said thoughtfully, "I don't think Paul was even born when The Greek died."

I said, "I rest my case," and we bumped fists.

Paul's face had gone the color of a pomegranate. And he took a swing at me! I boxed and I was fast and in shape and he wasn't and he was at a twelve-year forty-pound disadvantage and still he took a swing at me. I was sitting down and it was hard to know just what he had in mind. I leaned back to avoid being hit and grabbed his wrist with my right hand as it went by and gave it a good twist.

"You little son of a bitch!" he shouted. "Goddamned little son of a bitch!"

Philip got up and took hold of Paul's other elbow to pull him back into his chair and I let go of his wrist and damned if he didn't turn and take a swing at Philip. Philip was in pretty good shape and he was fast and what's more he'd also been a boxer and Paul had not, just a bully, and in about five seconds Philip had Paul on his knees with his head on his chair and one arm twisted up behind him.

Philip said, "Say it."

Paul said, "Fuck you!"

Andy and I were grinning.

Philip said, "Say it."

Paul muttered, "Okay," and Philip dropped his arm and stepped back.

Andy said, "He's still got it."

I said, "Yes he does."

Philip looked a little red in the face but it wasn't exertion, it was embarrassment.

Paul climbed the chair to his feet and walked out of the office, shrugging and straightening his jacket. The outer door slammed.

Andy said, "The meeting is adjourned."

I said to Philip, "Keep him away from me."

Philip said, "He and Lillian are going on a gambling cruise to the Bahamas for two weeks. That should cool him off. And you cool off, too."

"Are they taking Young Nicky?"

"No, he's staying with us."

"Good. They'd probably forget him on the dock."

Philip said, "We made a sizeable profit on your trip. You had some good wins out there. Very good. But he's had some losses recently. He's... feeling it."

Andy said, "Should I play that game at Kelly's tonight?"

Philip said, "Yes. You too, Sam."

Philip went into the outer office after Nick—Uncle Cy had already quietly disappeared—and Andy looked at me.

He said, "What just happened?"

I said, "I don't know, but I don't think I like it."

THURSDAY, NOVEMBER 26

I stayed home for a while. On Thanksgiving we had enough snow for me and Andy to take all the kids sledding at the golf course, at the end of which they thanked me in the traditional manner by all attacking me at once and stuffing snow down my back.

Then came the dead weeks between Thanksgiving and New Year's when all the players used up their money buying make-up baubles for their wives and girlfriends. Paul and Lillian came home from the Bahamas and left again the next day on a luxury guided tour of Racetracks of the South. They didn't even bother to stay home for Christmas and their young son Nicky joined Philip's household again, where he was happier and healthier and far better off.

2010
WEDNESDAY, JANUARY 6

Theophany. Three Kings Day. Epiphany. Take your pick. One of the Great Feasts of the Greek Orthodox calendar, and I went with my family. God and I had an on-again-off-again, chancy kind of relationship. He was in my good graces at the moment so I was there with a whole heart. My mind, however, was fractured.

Eleven months since February. Since Harry stood by the bar at Vincent's and introduced us.

"Frances Clare Russell, Sam Alexandros. Sam, Clare. Clare, Sam." He grinned at me. She was all but hidden by a thick muffler, a wool military greatcoat, and snowmobile boots. But there were those eyes. I pulled myself together.

Not my type.

I was pretty cocky about women. But not stupid. I didn't hit on adolescents, and I wondered what the hell Harry was doing with a fifteen-year-old.

Harry said, "We're going to a movie. Street Fighter—The Legend of Chun Li."

I said, "Christ, Harry, you have the worst taste in movies."

She said, "He does, but he buys me the popcorn with the butter," and for some reason made me laugh, and I watched them leave with a sudden jones on for popcorn.

February. 2009. Put it on his tombstone. Just the one date. It was either the beginning or the end of his life.

Two nights after he introduced us in the bar, Harry and I were driving back into the city from a game in a place called Afton and he said suddenly, "Play the thug with her and I'll kill you."

I had no intention of playing anything with her. No designs at all on whatever virtue she might have left. But Harry interested me. He seemed serious.

Harry was born and brought up in Bridgeport, maybe the roughest Irish neighborhood in Chicago. Maybe you don't even need to say 'Irish'. Made St. Paul's Rice Street look like a stroll in the park. His father owned a pub and a gang. Harry was a sharp-faced, black-hearted, black-eyed Black Irishman, my oldest friend outside the family, and he might very well try to kill me.

Who the hell *was* this woman?

I said calmly, "You aren't just another mild-mannered grad student, are you?"

He said, "No. Neither are you."

I said, "Is she yours?"

"No, God damn me for my sins, she's not." He was driving an old Jag that winter. He slapped his hand down on the shift knob, double-clutched, and dropped down a gear for the exit ramp. We roared around the corner and up Snelling and around another corner onto University, toward the Capitol. We were going for burgers at the Hmong's.

He said, "She came to a lecture I was giving about ethnography. The department has a lecture series every fall on the various sub-disciplines and the newest grad students get to give them. She came up afterward to ask me some questions about early photography in the field."

He came to a sudden stop and backed into a parking place.

He said, "She knew her stuff and she's gorgeous, so I asked her out. We did a couple of dates and I made a move on her and she froze up and started to shake. I liked her and I was getting laid elsewhere, so I backed off and we got to be friends." He laughed. "Six months later she told me that she was sixteen. Christ. I lit a candle to whoever stopped me. That was four years ago."

I said, "She still looks sixteen."

We got out and climbed over a snowbank to the sidewalk.

He said, "She needs a fucking guardian. She takes pictures. Really good pictures. Shockingly good. But she only sees the world that's through the lens. She reads people through the camera, gets inside their barriers—it's spooky. Scary. In my family we'd say *eldritch*. Outside the camera, her middle name is Oblivious and her call sign is KEEP AWAY."

We went in and sat down at the counter. The Hmong didn't have tables. It was a twenty-four-hour diner that had probably the best burgers in the city. At that time of the morning, after a game, maybe the best in the five-state area. The counterman and cook on the night shift was a middle-aged Hmong guy who slept in a chair at the end of the counter. He put the burgers on, went back to sleep, and always woke up at exactly the right second to flip them and again to take them off. We liked the show and figured he was working more than one job, maybe more than two, so we tipped him extravagantly.

Harry said, "Trouble with that is she has to be open, emotionally. All the time. Vulnerable. Exposed. She just got her degree—studio art—and she's getting out and about more and getting some attention from guys I don't like. Guys from Rice Street who've found Vincent's. She lived for a while with one of her professors and his wife, but now she's on her own."

I said, "I'm not in the angel business."

He said, "You are, because you're the only guy I can trust. We don't run her life, we just watch out for her."

"I don't watch out for women, I fuck them."

"Not this one."

A few nights later, still February, Vincent's again, warm and well-lighted, a big wooden table in the back room and eight or nine people around it, Clare among them, a long-lensed Nikon camera and a glass of dark beer on the table in front of her. And Harry again, hailing me. Me finding a chair next to her. Apparently she was drinking age. Out of the coat she was an attractive armful and she attracted me, and, with Harry looking amused and watchful, I set about charming her.

Without thinking, I made some remark, I don't remember it, and she giggled, a sound I would describe, if I had to, as enchanting, and she smiled at me, just at me, and I was so delighted that it showed on my face and Harry damn near fell off his goddamn chair laughing.

It was all there, all at once, wanting her, wanting her a lot, wanting possession.

The charmer charmed.

A little later she said she had to work and she slipped away.

The next day I told Harry, "All bets are off. If you think we have an alliance, you're wrong. We don't."

We were on our way to a game in a suburb of Rochester. Doctors live there. Doctors have lots of money. Hence the long drive. That's logic. Player's logic.

He didn't say anything for a while. Then he said, "I reserve the right to kill you."

I said, "Sure."

On our way home with about twenty grand each stashed about our persons, he said, "Sometimes you're out of town, sometimes I am." I was playing poker and he was doing fieldwork in Chicago—multi-generational Irish gangs. "Just pay attention."

I said, "I plan to."

I did. Looked for her and found her at the Rattle Rat, a funky coffeehouse near the U, where she worked. Conversations over coffee. A beer later at Vincent's. Long walks. Movies. Cautious approach toward friendship, often under Harry's watchful eye, interrupted by trips to play poker.

Then a long weekend, must have been Memorial Day. Harry was gone to Chicago on some family business (his father and uncle were still alive then and ran a lucrative fencing operation and money-laundering service out of the back of their pub), and she and I went for a long Sunday afternoon walk along the river and for supper at Wong's and I took her home and backed her up against the door to her little apartment and kissed her. Not a friendly kiss.

God *damn* but I wanted her. And she broke away, twisted her face aside, pushed on my shoulders.

I let go and turned and walked out, fast.

Harry knew. I don't know how he knew—I was pretty sure Clare hadn't told him—but she must have done or said *some*thing. If she'd actually told him, maybe he wouldn't have shot me, probably not, but he would have beat the shit out of me. His would have been the righteous anger and we both knew it.

So there were two or three weeks of Clare going out when I was coming in and Harry taking more of my money at the tables than I should be allowing, until finally one day I stopped Clare on the sidewalk outside the Rattle Rat and apologized. To a woman. A woman not related to me.

A new experience.

She smiled, first a bit tentatively and then happily, and we were back to friends.

I did pay attention then, and found out what I should have been paying attention to all along: she was terrified. All the time. She hid it very well, but both Harry and I could see it plain enough.

We didn't know, not then, why she was so full of fear, but of course I made some guesses. So did Harry, but he didn't know either. Why she chose to let me and Harry get close enough to be her bodyguards—Harry said it made him wonder if he was losing his scare factor—that was another mystery but she did, although I didn't know if she ever thought of us as bodyguards exactly.

She thought of us as friends. She wanted a friend. She craved a friend. I wasn't sure she'd ever had one before. She had a professor who mentored her and his wife who did some nurturing. She knew a lot of people when we went out to the bars. But no one she let in like she let me and Harry in.

Friends. Okay. That was what she needed, that was what she got.

Other men asked her out, and she allowed a couple of them to take her out and one that I knew of into her bed. My fingers itched to shoot them and so did Harry's but we held to watchful non-interference. He said, "Much as one might want to, one can't shoot everyone." Harry and I were twelve years older than Clare and we told each other that she needed to meet men her own age and maybe even sleep with them. But every man who came near her somehow got the message that we were watching and they knew: Fuck over Clare Russell and you are fucking with Sam Zandros and Harry Parker and *that* would be a mistake.

Did *she* know we were watching? I didn't know.

I was gone a lot that summer. Played at a string of resorts in Washington and Oregon and the Colorado Rockies and then an actual riverboat ride down the Mississippi. I tried to see Clare whenever I was in town, but she was busy too, making pictures. I wondered a lot, maybe even fantasized about whether Clare and I had any future together. But I was getting laid a lot and there didn't seem to be any hurry to make any sudden moves.

MONDAY, OCTOBER 25

Harry called me just before seven in the morning where I was. Six where he was. It had to be bad news.

He said, "Where are you?"

"Miami. Why?"

"Clare got married."

"What?"

"Clare got married."

"Who?"

"Donal O'Connell."

Christ. Not good news at all.

O'Connell was a slickie Irishman with an adorable accent who had first showed up one night about a month ago at Vincent's. Harry and his current cutie and Clare and I were having a quiet beer, and O'Connell barged in on our table on the grounds that Clare looked just like his poor dear dead sister in Dublin. Harry and I loathed him on sight. I went for more beers and he was in my spot when I got back, next to Clare, and playing up to her like she was holding his next paycheck. He accepted one of the beers though none of them were for him.

Harry said, "How soon can you be here?"

I was already at the airline's website. "I can catch a flight at ten. Lands at two-thirty."

"I'll be there."

He was there and I stuffed my bag behind the seat and jumped in. I said, "When did this atrocity take place?"

He sedately exited the airport roads, jumped from thirty to sixty and back to thirty through a negative time warp, did his fancy clutch maneuver, and we sped north on Hiawatha. "A week ago. I just found out about it, at a game at Elmore's. This morning. I haven't seen her for a few days."

"O'Connell was at Elmore's?"

He said, "No, he's not a player. It was Freddy Smith."

I said, "I heard O'Connell was getting friendly with the Smiths."

Harry said, "*I* heard that he *is* a Smith. Some sort of relative. Maybe he is."

I said, "Freddy told you she'd gotten married."

"He came late to Elmore's and told me that O'Connell had nabbed Zandros's pet bitch. Even married her, the dumb fuck. His words."

He shot across four lanes of traffic and onto an exit ramp.

I said, "You really should have helmets for your passengers in this thing."

He grinned briefly. "Enjoy it while you can. The asshole I won it from says he's got the cash to redeem it. I decided I'd rather have the money. It needs an engine rebuild."

I said, "Let's go straight to Clare's. Nobody else can answer our questions."

"And maybe we'll get a chance to beat the crap out of Donal."

I said, "One of my favorite negotiating techniques."

O'Connell answered the door, then stood in the opening, blocking our entry, right at home in a dingy T-shirt and saggy underpants.

I said, "We're here to see Clare."

"She ain't here."

We pushed on in and he tried for a gun that he was keeping on a nearby bookshelf. But Harry was by God fast and he had the gun in one hand and O'Connell's balls in the other before I had the door closed. The saggy pants offered no protection and plenty of room for a very comprehensive grip. O'Connell sucked in his breath and tried to stand on his tippy-toes and said, "Christ!" through his teeth. In ten seconds Harry had him face-down on the floor.

I yelled, "Clare!" and there was a small scuffling sound from the bedroom. I opened the door and went in.

She was crouched on the floor behind the bed, her arms wrapped around her knees and her face hidden.

I said, "Clare," and she looked up, peered out from under her lashes over the edge of the mattress, then lifted her face and I said, "Oh God."

Bruises and dried blood covered her lovely face and both her eyes were swollen and blackened. I came around the bed and lifted her to her feet and held her up against me. She acquiesced like a child. She was in a torn and filthy sleeveless white nightgown. The better to see the bruises all the way to her shoulders and the rope marks on her wrists. She started to shiver.

Harry shouted, "Bring me something to wrap this asshole up with."

I shouted back, "Lamp cords."

A small crash.

I pulled off my jacket and put it around her. Finally she said something, said, "Sam," and then she started to cry. I thought that was probably a good sign.

I said, "Come out to the other room."

She shook her head.

I put my arm around her shoulders. I said, "It's just Harry. No one else."

After a few seconds she nodded, still crying quietly. I urged her through the door.

This wasn't the duplex she was in later. This was a smaller apartment she had for a while after she graduated. One of those 1960s brick hives. Except for the small bedroom and bath, it was all one open living area. I held her as close to my side as I dared. When we came through the door, Harry was just finishing a very workmanlike knot in the lamp cord he was using on O'Connell's ankles. His wrists were already secured. Clare edged away from him.

Harry looked up and jumped to his feet. "Clare! Oh darlin'!"

O'Connell, who could move his mouth and not much else, yelled, "Don't say a word, you bitch. Keep your fookin' mouth shut!"

Harry kicked him in the face on his way to Clare, who he oh so gently embraced. Together we started her toward a large chair, but she hung back. "Not there," she managed. "His."

We got her to the couch and sitting, and Harry stripped off his jacket and put it over her knees. She huddled inside the jackets and we sat next to her, one on each side.

Harry said, "Hospital," but Clare said, "No. Please."

He bent and looked at her face. We both did. Her eyes were full of tears, and reddened and bruised, but there were no cuts, not even a split lip, just bruises. No, there was a cut, not big, behind her hairline and almost invisible but it had bled. And the black eyes. Her nose had been bloodied but not broken. The wrists were bruised and bloody, but there were no deep cuts, only skin scraped raw by whatever he had tied her up with. Then she lifted her head and I saw the bruising on her neck. Marks of a thin rope, or cord.

Harry said softly, "Any injuries we can't see? Inside?"

She said, "No, but—" She hesitated. "Here." She slowly and carefully moved Harry's jacket aside and lifted her nightgown to bare her left leg. There were three open sores on the inside of the thigh.

I said, also softly, "Burns?"

She nodded.

He tortured her. I went into the red zone, but stayed in control.

I said, "Anything else?"

She said, "No. No hospital. Please." She spoke so low I could hardly hear her.

Harry said to me, also very quietly, "I think we can take care of her. At least until we know we can't. We won't need a rape kit. There won't be any kind of trial."

I nodded. I said to Clare, "He's going to disappear. Forever. He'll never touch you again."

She took in a shuddering breath and nodded.

Harry said, "River?"

I said, "Swamps. North of the city."

"Good idea. I'll borrow a van. I know a guy."

Harry knew a lot of guys.

O'Connell started yelling and we stuffed his mouth with a dirty sock and taped it shut. He was looking wild-eyed mad but he was also looking scared. Good.

I said, "Let's put him behind the couch. Get him out of sight."

We did and then Harry ran a warm bath and helped Clare into it while I watched and yearned and held her robe. There were bruises all over her body—breasts, buttocks, back—some of them bite marks. Harry washed her carefully and dried her and she sat on a kitchen chair, huddled in her fleece robe and a pair of thick sox, and watched us work.

We bundled up O'Connell's clothes and personal stuff and all the used bedding and the rope fragments into a big hobo bundle and set it by the door to drop off at a far-away dumpster. His wallet was in the bedroom on the dresser. We pulled out all the money—just over a thousand bucks—and put it in Clare's handbag. We left everything else in the wallet.

We were about to add it to the bundle when Clare said, "Wait. Pawn ticket." And there was one, for a camera. Four fifty.

"Did he pawn anything else?" I asked.

"No."

"What was this?"

She whispered, "My new Nikon."

I said, "We'll get it back."

Harry said, "We're leaving fingerprints all over his stuff."

I said, "Yeah, we are. Fuck. Okay. Burn his papers. Any other stuff that can be identified—anything that takes prints but doesn't burn—wipe it, put it into a pillowcase, add a big rock, drop it in a river." We wiped his gun and put it in the sack with the wallet.

We got Clare dressed in a turtleneck T-shirt and a soft fleece warm-up suit and some athletic socks. Harry went off to borrow the van. I searched her bathroom cupboard and found a bottle of ibuprofen. In the kitchen there was a bottle of brandy. For later, I decided, and gave her some ibuprofen. I warmed up some chicken noodle soup for her, and she sat at the table and ate it slowly. She was swallowing around a sore throat, but the warm soup seemed to help.

Harry came back and brought some Chinese. Clare was able to eat a bit of tofu fried rice and drink a couple ounces of beer. Harry and I drank water.

Clare had an extra pillow and duvet in her closet and we tucked her up on the couch and she slept off and on.

O'Connell was quiet for the most part, but once he started trying to flop around and yell past the sock and the tape. Clare woke up like into a bad dream, but I knelt down and soothed her and Harry kicked O'Connell into submission again. Then he tied a long shoelace around Donal's neck. The bastard could breathe but just barely. If he didn't exert himself, like trying to yell.

Harry crouched by O'Connell, leaning close and smiling into O'Connell's face. "Ye'll have heard of the bogmen, Donal. Hundreds of years they've been in that bog water and almost good as new. Study them, the scientists do. So think about the contribution ye be making to science, two, three hundred years down the road. It's a grand thing ye be doin'." He stood and walked away, humming.

I said, "Who the hell are you channeling?"

"Me Uncle Sean, when he's in his cups. He subscribes to the Irish Journal of Anthropology in which I've had a couple of wee scholarly bits published, and he likes to discuss them when I go home."

O'Connell was moaning behind the duct tape.

We went on cleaning the apartment, getting rid of any and every visible trace of him. At midnight we rolled O'Connell into Clare's bedspread. He wiggled some, but he was pretty weak by then. Clare was struggling into a long loose anorak, another military surplus store special.

"I want to see," she said.

Harry and I looked at each other and I said, "Okay. But if we get stopped, you say we forced you to come."

She said, "No."

I said, "Yes. You promise."

She looked at both of us. We looked back. She said, "All right, I promise." She sounded almost petulant.

Harry took a black watch cap out of his pocket and pulled it down over her curls.

We drove for just under two hours, Harry driving, Clare in the front passenger's seat, me in the seat behind, O'Connell in the back under a tarp belonging to the owner of the van. The last part of the trip was all back roads. And dark.

At one point I said, "You know where we're going or are you just driving aimlessly?"

"I have a map." He patted where his shirt pocket was under his jacket. "The guy who owns this van hunts. And he owns some land up here that he hunts on. One day we were talking about hunting rituals and he told me about his land and about wild pigs." He had his voice pitched loud, so I could hear him in the back. "Feral pigs. Escapees from farms. They're a menace. You're allowed to shoot them on sight, no license required. They ruin the local vegetation and crops, even trees. And they have one trait that we are going to utilize. They'll eat anything—birds, small animals, big animals, whatever's there—and they are always ravenous. Two or three of them have encroached on his hunting land, and he knows they're there. We'll be on his land. Private, not public."

A weak keening sound came from under the tarp.

When we stopped we were at a place where the rutted primitive road ended abruptly at the edge of a swamp—low dense tangled trees, brownish water clogged with leaves and dead vegetation. Harry and I got out, looked around, and let the quiet settle in on us for a minute. Then we went to get O'Connell.

He didn't struggle. He wasn't being brave. Paralyzing fear had taken hold of him. His body had stopped functioning. He couldn't walk. His limbs were limp and he smelled of hot piss.

Clare opened her door and slid to the ground. She said, "I want him to see me."

Harry'd left the headlights on and he ripped the tape from O'Connell's eyes and mouth and put it in his own pocket, and we held him up so he could look at her. His eyes were terrible. She looked back at him and spat. Then we waded into the icy water, laid him face down in several inches of water, between some trees, and waded back out and watched. He wiggled and writhed convulsively for a short while, but didn't move for very long.

Harry said, "May God have mercy on your soul," and we got back into the van and Harry drove backward up the road until we could turn around. As we drove away I fancied hearing a piggy grunt behind us.

On the way back into the city, we disposed of the hobo bundle and the pillowcase, and while I cleaned up behind the couch where the late O'Connell had peed himself, and Clare dozed some more, Harry returned the van and came back with groceries. I fixed breakfast and we sat and ate and Clare started talking.

She said, "It was for immigration. He wanted to get a green card and he said that he could if he married a U.S. citizen. He said it would be just a formality, not a real marriage, and we would get a divorce later. He said he had to live here for a while to make them think it was real. He was going to give me some money—five thousand dollars he said—and I thought I could help him." Her head was down. "I was so stupid."

Harry said, "No you weren't. Maybe a little gullible."

She said, "He made it seem so... simple. So plausible."

She picked up a piece of toast and ate one corner and started to tear the rest of it into little pieces. She said, "He was... funny, sort of... clownish, and he made me laugh and at first he was, I guess, well, gentle. Just some little hugs and kisses and... not pushy or anything. And then he wanted to make it real."

I said, "To have sex."

"He called it fooking." She drank some juice. "And I said no."

Harry said, "And the son of a bitch beat you up and tied you down and raped you. Or maybe not in that order. Maybe he had to tie you down before he could beat you up."

She nodded. Tears were dripping into her wretched little pile of toast bits. She said, "Why are you doing all this?"

I said, "We're your friends."

She nodded again. She said in a voice that seemed almost to be strangling her, "Thank you."

Harry said, "Any chance you're pregnant?"

She looked up, shock on her face.

He brought out a small box that said PLAN B on it. "Take this now," he said, and handed it to her. She took the box and read the label.

She said, "It says three days."

I said, "Has it been longer?"

"I don't know. I sort of lost—when I was—you know—"

I said, "Tied down? It was for days?"

She whispered, "Yes."

Harry said, "Just take the pill. If there's more to deal with later, we'll deal with it."

I said to Harry, "You have a big supply of those?"

He grinned. "Right next to the condoms."

She ripped open the box, extracted the pill, and swallowed it with cold coffee.

She said, "I can't go out."

I said, "Not until you want to. When you feel comfortable. One of us will stay here with you as long as you need."

"I don't want to live here anymore."

Harry said, "Now is probably not a good time to be talking to prospective landlords."

"No. I guess not."

I said, "Do you want to go to a shelter? Or to your professor's?"

"No. Never mind. I'll stay here."

Harry said, "We'll do a cleansing ceremony."

And we did. A Native American smudge. First we spent the rest of the morning cleaning her apartment from top to bottom, working at erasing every molecule of O'Connell from the place. Then I sat with Clare on my lap on the couch while she cried some more and slept some more, and I thought about—her—and Harry went out to acquire what we needed: a large feather, a braid of an herb called sweetgrass, some wooden kitchen matches, and a shallow dish-shaped shell. Abalone, he said.

Harry said, "This is the easiest cleaning ritual I know, and all the elements are easy to get. I know a guy. A shaman. He's an instructor in the department." He opened three windows, "For the smoke to escape and take the negative energy with it."

Clare watched him intently.

He was very serious. I would even say respectful. He lit a length of the braided herb in the shell, then damped it down to put out the flame but leave it smoking. Using the feather he wafted the smoke over himself, then over Clare, and then me. Then we walked through the house while he directed smoke in every direction, every corner, of every space. Her bed was stripped to the bare mattress, and we'd turned it over, and he paid particular attention to sending the smoke all over it. He went out into the front and rear halls and down the stairs. He went into the parking lot and smudged the interior of her car. Once I heard him muttering to himself. We followed him everywhere, Clare clutching my hand.

He said, "Walk through and tell me if there are any places that need more cleansing."

She walked solemnly through and came back shaking her head. "He's gone," she said.

Harry burned the map to the dump-site in the kitchen sink and washed the ashes down the drain.

We stayed with her, one or both of us, for three weeks, until her bruises were only memories. Harry got her a big jar of arnica ointment for the bruising and some other stuff for the burns and the raw skin from the ropes and she rubbed it on. We got her all new bed linens and towels. We got rid of her mattress and the couch and the upholstered chair that O'Connell had sat on in his underwear and replaced them. We cleaned the refrigerator and the stove and scrubbed and waxed the floors. I cooked and we stocked her up good with new groceries.

Behind some books Harry found an envelope containing O'Connell's passport and some papers. The papers were a marriage license application downloaded from some website in Iowa and a marriage license ditto signed by the Reverend Larry Waters. The application was filled in but there was no indication it had ever been filed in any office of any government.

Harry said, "Where did this ceremony take place?"

She said, "At that man's office. It's a storefront church, over on the east side."

We all drove there and parked about a block away. She and I watched Harry go to the side door that said Office and talk to someone and come back to the car.

"It's all bullshit," he said. "Larry Waters does the janitorial work."

I thought she was going to choke from laughing.

We burned the papers and the passport.

She started having bad dreams. Harry smudged again and she slept soundly.

He told me, "It's as good as hypnosis."

I said, "Maybe it *is* hypnosis."

He said, "I don't really have an opinion on that one."

Finally we took her for a few beers at Vincent's. Before we left I said, "It was all a silly joke that some idiot took seriously and made into a rumor. A story that was going around. You've been working a lot and not going out because you had the flu. You haven't seen O'Connell for weeks. And that last part is true."

She said, "Okay," and it was.

I told Andy about it but no one else. Life went back to normal.

MONDAY, NOVEMBER 29

She started her portrait studio. She already sold her freelance work—
mostly outdoor urban spaces with no people in them, often taken
at night—by pinning it to the walls in coffee shops and bookstores
and one small gallery, but to concentrate on portraits she needed a place.

It was also then that I first really saw her pictures. *Saw* them. She
had had a few on her walls at the little apartment, but I hadn't paid them
much attention. I was fond of or had been beguiled by or challenged by
many photos that I saw and I saw many because I was a heavy reader of history, but now I sat and looked at hers, and thought about the
art courses I'd taken, and wondered why hers were so good. Thought
back to the pictures in those big heavy textbooks. Took all the nieces
and nephews to the library and brought home books of photographs by
Lange and Bourke-White and Evans and Rothstein. Went to the book
stores and bought a dozen books and then did it again. I didn't tell her.

She rented the upstairs of an old duplex in one of the University
neighborhoods called the Flatlands for more than she could really af-
ford and started cleaning and painting everything white. Harry and I did
some gypsy plumbing for her darkroom. He knew how and I helped.
And we took her out to eat a lot so she could pay her rent.

The duplex had been built as a single-family, so all her rooms had
been bedrooms. She used the room overlooking the street as her studio,
and the middle room as living room and office. Then came two bedrooms, one behind the other, and the front one, off the living room, be-

came the darkroom-slash-work-room. Off to the other side of the house she had a small kitchen and a big bathroom, with a separate shower and the biggest old clawfoot tub I'd ever seen.

The living room had a couch, but it was also her office and waiting room, with a big forties-style government-surplus gray steel desk and swiveling desk chair and a file cabinet at the far end, some bookshelves, and four wooden straight-back chairs lined up in front of the bookshelves, across from the couch. There was a small TV on one of the bookshelves.

The only things on the walls were the dozen or so photographs she was currently looking at. Sometimes her own work, sometimes pictures torn from magazines or old books that she dug out of the bookstore's sub-basement. Once I stopped her just as she was about to rip up Let Us Now Praise Famous Men. It was a first edition, 1941, and a first printing, in quite good shape. I told her I'd buy her another, which I did, one that was missing several pages of text but had all the photos, for her to dismember to her heart's content.

She'd leave them up for days or weeks, then change one or several or all, putting up others to live with for a while.

As soon as I got my master's in my hand, with Harry and Clare in the audience applauding wildly, on the opposite side of the auditorium from my family, I was traveling more, in and out of town, bringing home a lot of money and getting laid plenty. I thought about becoming the poker player with the PhD and decided no. Maybe when I needed something to do in my old age.

I'd come back into town and she'd look up from a camera and smile and say, "Hi!" and we'd go out for movies and beers and talk. If she had time. Her studio was quickly successful, her portraits much in demand. She had an uncanny talent.

2011
Sunday, July 3

I tried once more. I sat across from her in a booth at Vincent's and leaned on the table and put my hands on hers, held them, like little prisoner birds. She stiffened and slowly, not looking at me, pulled hers away. I stared at her lovely face and decided I was crazy to go on like this. The next day I went to LA and stayed there. It was a late evening flight out of town and the night was very clear. We watched fireworks displays from above all along the route.

SUNDAY, SEPTEMBER 11

1

I did very well in the Glitter City. Sent lots of money back to St. Paul while I lived comfortably in a residence hotel. Two rooms and a small but nicely furnished kitchen and good room service and a good restaurant and a pool. A very accommodating blondie who worked in a car dealership and lived just down the hall. We met at the pool and Uncle Cy vetted her for me the first time I took her out to dinner. I went to the beach a lot and ate well and swam and ran and worked out and read a lot of books and kept myself under the radar. I was bored silly, but the blondie was close-to-hand and I was too lazy—or something—to look elsewhere for a woman to take home to my sister.

2

Clare sent me a text message:

> *sam are you stikll in la there ir something happening here but idon't know what it is harry irs gone somewhere can you bcallme clare*

Of course I can call you Clare. And where are the Marx Brothers when you need them.

I was surprised she even knew how to send a text message. She hadn't figured out how to punctuate. Maybe hadn't taken the time. That was sort of disturbing in itself.

I had gotten the message just as I was arriving at the house in South Pasadena to which I'd been invited for a friendly Sunday evening game. I stood in the driveway and tried to call her, then tried to call Harry. No answer at either one, and then Ken Miller drove up and seemed to expect me to walk in with him.

3

"Action's on you, Mr. Zandros."

I jerked back to the card room to say, "Call."

Where the hell is Harry? If Harry hasn't seen her, at least he'll have heard what's going on. Is she in trouble? For Christ's sake, she could have said.

There is something happening here but I don't know what it is

One could say she never knows what's happening but one would be wrong.

Can you call me

Yes, I can call you. Of course I can call you.

"Call."

Or I can go home and find out for myself.

I took some money away with me from the game. Less than usual, maybe, but enough to feel like I was earning my keep. Ken Miller and I stopped in a little bar and drank a couple of early Monday morning whiskies with the shaky alcoholics and said so long for now and I'll see you.

I stuffed everything into my large duffel and my carry-on, left tips for all the hotel staff, slipped a note under the blondie's door, checked out, returned my rental car, and took the shuttle to the airport.

MONDAY, SEPTEMBER 12

1

The last red-orange rays of the sun still lit up the inside of the 787 as we made the long shallow approach over flat Midwestern farmland into Minneapolis-St. Paul, but the ground under us was already dark and the streetlamps were lighting up the differences between the two cities.

The larger one, Minneapolis, was both the western of the two cities and a western city, built on a grid, straight lines and right angles, except where the river pushed through its own inexorable plan. The eastern city, St. Paul, was curving lines of lights following narrow winding streets that came together every which way, and straight lines of lights that came together at odd angles, sometimes several at once.

I'd heard it called the westernmost eastern city, but that sounded a bit overblown.

I was traveling executive and sitting alone, and I got the pretty attendant to give me two mini-bottles of scotch and some ice. She also gave me the eye several times on her way up and down the aisle. Black jeans, short boots, blue dress shirt, black Italian-cut sport coat—maybe she thought I was a movie star traveling incognito.

But I was tired. Too tired to smile back any more than perfunctorily. Being away from home for so long was wearing me down.

Tired but not sleepy. I spent most of the trip staring out the window at the clouds chasing us and thinking about the itchy restlessness that had been plaguing me in Los Angeles. And about Clare. Was it Clare plaguing me? Yes.

2

The sunset overtook the day and we landed in inky darkness. Home again, home again, jiggety jog.

I flexed my shoulders and decided that, with some reservations, I was glad to be back.

From the cab I called Philip.

I said, "I'm in St. Paul."

He said, "You are."

"Landed forty minutes ago. I probably won't be home until tomorrow."

"I'll tell Catherine. Anything else I should know now?"

"No. I'll be in the office tomorrow."

I paid off my taxi in front of Clare's duplex. The outer door lock was still broken. I found the hall light switch, but nothing happened when I flipped it and I said, "Damn it." I felt my way toward the stairs and kicked something soft. I said, "*Damn* it!"

What I'd thought was a shadow was a person, a man, on the floor, half propped against the wall, slumped onto the bottom step. I bent and tried to see his face in the gloom but couldn't, grabbed a shoulder and shook it and said, "Hey! Hey, buddy." Then I felt the looseness in the shoulder joint and said, "Oh, shit." I touched the neck. There was no need to try to find the pulse, he—it—was too still, too limp, too... lifeless, but I tried anyway. No luck. I straightened and backed off and stepped in something liquid. Sticky. I went up the stairs, thinking that I must be leaving footprints.

I knocked on her door and called her name. "Clare. It's Sam."

The door came open on the chain. "Sam! You're in Los Angeles. Well, obviously not, but you were. Weren't you?"

"Yeah. Let me in." I kicked off my boots to leave them on the landing.

The door went shut, the chain rattled, and I pushed on it impatiently, swinging it wide.

"Did you just come back?" she asked, moving to the side as I walked in. I stopped in the middle of the room and dropped my duffel bag and stood and looked at her. Relaxed into the pleasure of it.

Full round breasts and nicely round bottom and slender waist. Longish legs. Slim-hipped long-legged small-waisted—I had spent a lot of time thinking about that body. I hoped I could get her through this.

"Is something wrong?" she asked.

"You okay?" I asked back.

She said, "Yes. Hi."

I said, "Hi. There's a body in the hallway. Downstairs."

"A what?"

"A body. Somebody dead."

She looked blank. "Who?"

I shook my head. "Don't know. The fucking light's burned out. You better call the cops. 911." I bent to unzip my duffel bag and pull out a pair of athletic shoes. "I'll go down and wait for them. You stay here."

I stuffed my feet into the shoes and went back out the door.

I'd been on the porch for eight minutes when I heard the first sirens. I was hunched into a raincoat that had been fine for Los Angeles but was too light for a cold rainy night in September in St. Paul, and when the first patrol car arrived I followed the two cops into the hallway and staked out an observation post several steps up.

Clare came down carrying a Nikon. She'd put on a heavy sweater and she stood at my back, one step up, and peered over my shoulder and said nothing, but made a faint, shocked sound when a powerful flashlight swept over the face of the dead man and then gleamed on the dark surface of the blood puddled under him. I heard the shutter sound as the flashlight beam swept back the other way.

I turned my head and talked low. "You know him?"

She said, "No."

I said, "I do."

3

The plainclothes cops arrived. Someone had brought in a garishly bright lamp on a tall stand, and the hallway was flooded with ugly light. The first detective in the door was a middle-aged, middle-sized guy with a reddish face and dirty-blond hair, in a wrinkled cheap suit, who gave me raised eyebrows, said, "Well, shit. Sam Zandros," and joined us on the stairs.

I showed some teeth. "Hello, Denny."

"Knew I'd see you at a crime scene sooner or later."

I showed more teeth. He looked at Clare.

I said, "Clare Russell. She lives here." To Clare, "Denny Linden."

"Sergeant Dennis Linden," Linden said. He took out his ID and flipped it open for us. "You live upstairs or downstairs?" he asked her.

"Upstairs."

Linden went back down and leaned over the body.

I felt her steady her arm on my shoulder and heard the snap and buzz. Linden heard it too and looked back.

She tilted her head at the scene below. "Would it be—could I photograph this? What you're doing?"

Linden frowned.

I said, "She's a pro."

"Newspaper?"

"Portraits."

Linden shrugged. "Stay on the steps." Another detective was watching the police photographer record the scene, waiting his turn at the body. Clare wedged herself between me and the wall, steadied an arm on my shoulder. I took in her warmth and the softness of her breast. The police photographer heard her camera, glanced up, and went back to his work. He was using a flash and Clare's camera clicked again just as his flash triggered. I heard her let out her breath and looked around at her.

"Got it," she whispered.

Linden said to me, "You know him?"

I said, "Gordy Terrell."

"Friend of yours?"

I said, "No. Saw him around."

"Know anything about him?"

"No."

"*Hear* anything about him?"

"A little."

"What'd you hear?" Linden asked.

"I heard he was a sort of chaperone, for some girls. Went to parties with them, that sort of thing."

Linden grunted. "Chaperone, huh?"

I shrugged.

A young assistant coroner, wearing a raincoat over scrubs, was examining the body. Clare lowered her camera for a moment, cleared her throat, and lifted it again. She put her back to the wall and pointed the camera at the body and clicked off three shots. Then she pushed past me and went down two steps. The police photographer sidled over to stand by her, and they introduced themselves and compared notes in low voices.

"He come here to see you?" Linden asked me.

"Not likely. I've been out of town. My plane just landed two hours ago. Nobody knew I was coming back, not even my brothers."

"Miss, uh, Russell?"

"No."

"Did she know Terrell?"

I blew out a breath, thought about saying how the hell would I know? But it was Clare. "No."

"Who lives there?" Linden jerked his head at the door to the downstairs apartment.

"Couple guys. I've never seen them."

"They don't seem to be home. So maybe Miss Russell was the only one on the premises when Gordy got it."

I looked at the back of Clare's head and held onto my temper. "You're forgetting the one who got Gordy. And Gordy, of course. He was here."

Linden shifted his weight. "Let's go upstairs," he suggested.

I put out a hand and touched her arm.

As we started up, Linden said, "These your footprints?"

Clare looked down, then up at me, her distress clear on her face. "Yeah."

"We'll need your shoes."

I stopped on the upper landing and pointed to my boots. Leather-lined, very comfortable. I liked them, I'd never see them again.

Linden gestured at the brass plate on the door. "Who's Frances Russell?"

Clare said, "I am. Frances Clare Russell."

He motioned for Clare to go into the apartment and then me, and he followed us.

She said, "Please. Sit down."

Linden looked around, went to the couch and sat. Clare sat down on one of the wooden straight chairs and I sat in her desk chair. He said accusingly to Clare, "This is where you have your business?"

She just said, "Yes."

"Where do you live?"

"Here."

Linden didn't look tired, exactly, but he looked fed-up, and sour, and that made him look older than I knew he was. Clare lifted the camera and took two quick shots of him frowning at her speculatively. Then he smiled, still sour, and she got that, too.

"Would you like some coffee?" she asked.

Linden said, "No, thanks." He took a small spiral-bound notebook and a ballpoint pen from his inner pocket, and held them at the ready. "Did you know the victim?"

She shook her head. "No."

"Did you ever see him before?"

"No."

"Maybe when you were out with Sam? At a party? A bar?"

"No."

"You seem very sure."

She shrugged. "I remember faces."

Linden let his gaze rest on a portrait on the wall opposite the couch, a young boy wearing a clown suit but no makeup, grinning happily at the camera.

"How did he... die?" she asked Linden.

"Stab wound in the neck. Just right of center. His right. Hit an artery."

I jerked open the top drawer of Clare's desk, rummaged inside until I found her letter opener. I held it out to her. "Here. Get up."

Linden just watched.

"Come on, get up. Take this."

She stood and took it, looking back and forth at Linden and me.

"It's a knife," I said. "Stab me with it."

"What?"

"Attack me. Stab me. Kill me."

"Sam..."

"Do it!"

She turned the letter opener in her right hand, grasped the hilt, started to raise it above her shoulder, obviously thinking back to some movie scene —

I brought up my left hand and grabbed her right wrist. With my right hand I took the opener from her. I tossed it on the desk and looked at Linden, that rat bastard, who just shrugged.

4

Everyone was gone. Linden and the supporting cast. The body.

No media showed up.

I put my coat and jacket on a hook on the back of Clare's door and found a sweater in my duffel and put it on. I went into the kitchen, shook the coffeepot to gauge its contents, and turned on the gas fire under it. She followed me. I opened the refrigerator.

I found a plastic bag of carrots and celery, a carton of orange juice, three containers of yogurt, and a whole-wheat bagel.

I said, "Can I eat your bagel?"

She said, "Sure," and I took the bagel and closed the refrigerator.

I asked, "Can I stay here tonight?"

"Sure."

"You seeing anybody?" The bagel was dry, but it was something to chew on.

"No."

"Just tonight?"

"At all."

That was good news. "Do you have any money?"

"A little." She leaned on the sink, her arms folded across her middle.

I said, "Let's go out for a drink."

"Don't you have any money?"

"I bought a plane ticket and two drinks and a ride in a cab and I have sixteen dollars." Well, a little more, but hundreds didn't count in this life.

"They have this wonderful new invention, the ATM. You put a little piece of plastic into it and it gives you money."

"Yeah, well, you're supposed to have money in the machine before you put the plastic in." I'd all but emptied my personal account that morning. "And I despise the whole idea."

"Luddite."

"Are you broke?" I demanded.

"I can probably buy another bagel."

I shrugged. "Tomorrow I'll see my brothers."

"And tonight we drink."

"Yes."

She said, "Okay. But not Vincent's."

"No. Not there. Any gas in your car?" I poured and drank coffee. It was lukewarm and terrible. I dunked the bagel. That produced a wet chewy bagel saturated with terrible coffee. I led the way back into the living room, bagel in hand, and sat in her desk chair again.

She followed and sat where she had before. "A little. Enough."

"You're working."

"I was." Several contact sheets and a magnifying glass were laid out under a strong lamp on her desktop. "I'd just as soon quit for the night." But she made no move to get out of the chair.

I said, "Come on. I know a place."

She held out her hand and I put the bagel into the coffee cup and the cup down on her desk and took the hand and pulled her to her feet.

5

We went to a place I knew named Bron's. I drank there sometimes when I didn't want—anything. The bartender gave me a lifted hand as we came in and the waitress gave me a smile.

Clare said, "You've been here before."

I said, "It's... quiet."

It was very quiet. The jukebox was on but the music was cool modern piano jazz and the volume was low. Conversation was at a minimum, even at a table in the back where six men were playing cards. Two of the card players nodded at me and one lifted a hand, but none of them spoke.

Our drinks came—my Johnnie Black and water and Clare's Sam Adams, which was what they had on tap. I paid. Clare drank some and sighed and I could see her let down a little. Then she said, "Does that Sergeant Linden think I killed that man?"

I glared at her. "No, he doesn't. It's on his list of desirable outcomes, but there are several above you. Like me."

They had taken my boots away in a plastic bag—I hoped I'd never see them on some cop's feet—and looked at Clare's kitchen knives—"*Not*," she said, "a matched set of ten with one in the middle missing thank *God*!"— and searched the trash and the yard and the street and the alley and the yards next door. The young men downstairs had come home, and had loudly asserted shock and ignorance. Linden had asked to search Clare's apartment and she'd said yes, but the search had seemed cursory.

I grinned at her. "You lied to Denny, didn't you? You'd seen Gordy Terrell before."

"Of course. At Vincent's. But I didn't know who he was or what he did."

"So you didn't lie to me, then."

I'd said do you know him? And she'd said no.

She said, "I'd seen him. I didn't think it was... relevant."

"It's not. So just hold that thought if Denny comes back."

"Will he?"

I said, "Probably. He wants to find a string to pull on that has me at the other end."

"You showed him your airline ticket," she said. "It's got all those times and things on it. Numbers. Codes. And they can find the flight attendant. If it's a female, she's sure to remember you. And the cab driver—they must have records, at the cab company."

"Yeah, but they don't fingerprint the passengers. Yet. The times could be close. Terrell was rather newly dead when I arrived, I think. The blood was still, uh, liquid."

She said, "I'm a *much* better suspect. I was right upstairs—I must have been there when—when—"

She choked a little and suddenly she was crying. I moved from my side of the booth to hers and put my arms around her. She hid her face against my shoulder, and I let my cheek rest on her hair.

She said in a raspy whisper, "Oh *God*, Sam, what if they *arrest* me?"

"They won't. Even Denny Linden has to have *some* evidence. He'll find out what happened. If he doesn't, maybe I will."

"How will you do that?"

"I think I probably know almost as many bad guys as he does. Maybe one of them will tell me."

"Do you have a handkerchief?"

I did, a clean one even, and I gave it to her. She mopped her face and blew her nose. I kept my arms around her and she leaned on me.

I said, "Tell me about the text message."

She didn't speak.

I said, "I tried to call you back."

She said, "I wasn't answering my phone. I—couldn't." Another hesitation. "I had a few dates with Barry Salter."

"Yeah?"

"Probably a mistake."

"Yeah."

"He wanted to go to bed with me and I said no and told him I didn't want to see him anymore."

There would be more to it than that but it could wait.

She said, "Barry was—he was very angry. He called me a couple of times. On Saturday. I stayed Saturday night and last night with the Cochrans."

"What're you doing back home? Did you tell Harry?"

"I couldn't reach him. I had to come home today to work."

"What did Salter say? On the phone."

"Just, he wanted to talk to me. He said he didn't mean to be... pushy. I just shouldn't... make him angry."

"Right. Your fault." Bastard. "What's happening that you don't understand?"

"I don't know. If I understood it—"

"Right."

She sighed. "Twice we were in Vincent's and he went to talk with some men, two of them, in another booth, someone I'd never met, I'm sure of it, and they—they kept looking at me. They looked at me and waved and laughed. They were—I don't know why exactly, but they were scary. Sort of."

"And you'd never seen them before."

"I'm sure of it."

"Okay." I believed her. Faces.

"I asked him, who were those guys you were talking to. He said some Rice Street guys. He said they just think it's pretty funny, you going out with me. Meaning me and him. They said maybe Zandros ain't so tough after all. But I didn't really believe that was why they were laughing. I think he made that part up."

"Did he say their names?"

"Just one. He said, that's Freddy Smith in the hat. Like I should be impressed. But I'd never heard of him."

I had. Kevvy Smith's cousin. I said, "Barry's pond is pretty small."

"And he kept asking me about you."

"Asking what?"

"Where you played cards. Who did you play with. How much money did you make. Were you still out of town. Where were you."

"What did you tell him?"

"Nothing! I didn't *know* anything. Harry told me you were still in Los Angeles. But I didn't tell Barry that. It was none of his business."

"Right."

She said, "You were gone a long time."

I really didn't have anything to say to that.

I knew who Salter was but I hadn't thought he was anything but a bottom-feeding thug who made his living fleecing immigrants, selling them very suspect used cars. He'd asked me to play a couple of times, but I declined. I didn't know what other interest he might have in me. Except maybe to pass on gossip about me to Freddy to pass on up the line to Freddy's cousin Kevvy.

She was leaning in more, going limp. She asked, "What was that act with the letter opener?"

"A little demonstration that you don't know the first thing about knife fighting."

"Like what?"

"You held it wrong, to start with. That overhand style went out with Lon Chaney. And any kid on the street could take it away from you in a half minute."

"Did he know that?"

"Yeah."

"He didn't seem too impressed."

"Cops his age are not easy to impress."

"I could have been putting you both on."

I said, "Yeah, right."

6

Someone had more or less cleaned up the blood in the hall, and there was now a working bulb in the light fixture. The better to see the large black stain on the floor.

"I'm calling your landlord about the front door lock tomorrow," I said, feeling growly.

Clare hurried past the stain and up the stairs. When we got inside the apartment she shot the deadbolt home and fumbled the chain lock into place.

"Hang on," I said. I went around the apartment checking the locks on all the windows and doors, and came back to find Clare standing where I had left her, in the middle of the living room, clutching herself around her middle. I put my arms around her, pinning her arms between us, and felt her trembling.

She said, "Thank you."

"Yeah."

After a moment I let her go. She brought her extra quilt and pillow from the bedroom closet, and I sat down on the couch to take off my shoes.

"I'm glad you're back," she said, and went rather quickly into the bedroom.

"Yeah," I said, after she'd closed the door. "Me too."

TUESDAY, SEPTEMBER 13

1

In the morning I made coffee—twice, because she knocked the grounds into the sink the first time—and she turned her back on me and ate strawberry yogurt. When she turned back her eyes were red and wet.

"I hate this," she said. "Dead bodies and nasty cops and being scared. Those guys downstairs are never home. They're no help."

She picked up the coffeepot and swung it around and hit it against the side of the refrigerator. I took it out of her hand and poured two cups. She took one.

"Have you ever been faithful to any woman?" she asked suddenly.

"Jesus, what kind of question is that, first thing in the morning?"

"So, no."

"It never mattered. What're you doing today?"

"I have six clients scheduled."

I said, "A heavy day."

"Yes." There was a strong note of satisfaction in her voice.

"Good. Meet me at Vincent's at six. Will you be done by then?"

"I should be."

I said, "If I'm not there, wait. I'll buy dinner."

"I thought you were broke."

"I'll be seeing my brothers today."

A few minutes later she followed me down the stairs. Someone had thrown a rug over the stain. The rug was off-center in the hallway, but I resisted the urge to move it.

We went out of the house, onto the porch, and she stood with me in the thin sunlight while I lit a small cigar.

"That smells good in the open air," she said.

"It better, the price I pay for them."

She laughed and put her hands in her pockets and looked out into her quiet street. "It feels strange," she said.

I said, "It'll be okay. I'll see you at six. Lock your door, please."

She nodded, and then I went down the steps to the street, and when I looked back at the end of the block, she was still watching me walk away.

2

I was in a back-room booth at Vincent's with Harry, drinking Guinness and eating pretzels. We were both in cool-weather garb—T-shirt, jeans, low hiking boots, unbuttoned flannel shirt with sleeves rolled up (me) and hoodie with sleeves pushed up (him)—showing our muscular, tanned forearms—and a couple of young co-ed cuties were giving us the sweet eye.

Harry gave one of them a long speculative look and she turned away, flustered.

"Where you been?" I asked him.

"Spent the weekend on the North Shore with a young lady of my acquaintance who's into trees. Lots of trees there. Very pretty. We discussed my Druid ancestors. How'd you know I was gone?"

"Clare texted me. Said she'd tried to get hold of you."

"She texted you? She knew how?"

I said, "Well, sort of. Punctuation was beyond her."

He said, "What was so urgent?"

"She didn't know. She said something was going on here and she didn't know what it was."

He said, "You've seen her."

I said, "Yeah. You heard the news."

"Yeah. Glad you were there. Is that what was going on?"

"I'm not sure." I told him what she told me about Barry Salter and his bar buddies.

He said, "She texted you." He shook his head. "She must have been more scared than usual."

"Yeah. Any good games around?" I asked.

"Kelly's. Jenneky's, of course. Elmore's. Same old. There's that bar—the Whiskey Tree—over on University. There've been some rich games there. But I get bad feelings, so I'm not going there no more. I think it's a training school for mechanics, and I don't think they're quite discreet enough for my tastes. Too many druggies, both buying and selling. You here to stay? Back on the circuit?"

"Yeah." I ate a pretzel.

He said, "So three months didn't work?"

"No."

"Going to try for six?"

"Waste of time."

He said, "I saw her here last Wednesday. She looked as luscious as ever. I was thinking of having an affair with her."

I said, "I have a gun and I could shoot you with it."

He smiled and said, "So do I."

I said, "Was she with anyone?"

He said, "Barry Salter. You should shoot him."

"Someone should. But she told me she wasn't seeing him anymore."

"Good."

I said, "Yeah. Very."

"So when the fuck," he said, just a little challengingly, "are you going to get off the goddamn dime and get the lady into the House of Alexandros?"

I was silent.

He sighed. "We talked for a few minutes. About you. She said Salter kept talking about you, wanting to play cards with you, said you'd never do it. Said he knew guys would kick your ass. I said you and I both play poker pretty regularly and I wouldn't play with Salter either. She didn't seem to know about the cards."

"You know how she is. She knows. But she never asks. She wouldn't even know what to ask. What she knows about cards you could inscribe on your thumbnail. Maybe she's not interested enough."

"And you never say. Fuck. But I'm glad you're back. Some of those guys around Salter creep *me* out."

"I wish she had better—judgment about who she—" I stopped. That sentence didn't seem to be going anywhere I wanted to go.

Harry said, "She's too busy thinking about other things to notice what losers they are. They ask her out, they chat her up, and she thinks they're the nice guys they're impersonating. She said once that O'Connell made her laugh. And they're too stupid to notice that her mind is wandering. They think she must be a mink because you are who you are. And then there's the thrill of baiting the guard dog, you being the Doberman."

"Harry…"

"Let me finish this, I'm on a roll. Here's the part you keep forgetting. You're the real thing, Sam, and they're not, but maybe that's how she tries for what she wants. That she ain't gettin'. There's really only one man on her mind, Sam. You know that." He was quiet for a moment. "I loved her so much when she was sixteen but she wasn't for me. She wasn't for anyone then. So I figured you could be the one and I was right. But God I wish it could have been me."

"Jesus, Harry."

We sat for several moments, not talking, getting our cool back.

"It's time, man. Before someone like me decides *you* are just not interested enough. Or one or God forbid several of those guys around Salter decide she's for grabbing. See the light, boy. She could be in trouble."

3

I made the decision while we stood outside the front door of the bar and waited for our heads to clear out a bit.

I said, "Time Barry and I had a talk."

"Yeah?"

"Want to come with? You can drive."

"Sure."

We trotted across the street and got into his car. An old Porsche.

He said, "Where do you think he is?"

"Let's try that used car dump he works at."

He started the car and made an illegal left turn onto University Avenue in front of a bus.

He said, "You playing at Kelly's tonight?"

"Yeah."

"I heard Kelly brought in a couple of big dogs from Chicago."

I smiled. "Replenishing the local money supply?"

He said, "Yeah. Nice guy, that Kelly."

We crossed the city limits into St. Paul, and the look of the storefronts changed immediately. They call them the Twin Cities, but they're fraternal at best.

He made several screeching turns and did a lot of shifting and crossed the river and we were on Lake Street. The street of dreamers still holding on by their fingernails.

He said, "What about Kevvy? I mean, after we beat the shit out of Barry."

I said, "He ain't Barry's daddy. My guess? He'll let Barry take a beat-down as an object lesson to his other guys not to be free-lancing. If there's something going on, he wants us for his own self."

He said, "You think Kevvy knows what 'object lesson' means?"

I said, "Maybe he doesn't know what to call it, but he sure as hell knows what it is."

He said, "Are we beating the shit out of Barry today?"

I said, "Let's just see what presents itself."

He turned a corner and parked the car, and we got out and walked back. The lot was to our right and we could see Barry lounging against a fender while he listened to a Hispanic guy who didn't speak much English. As we approached he lost interest in the Hispanic guy and watched us instead.

Barry, who was everyone's idea of a five-foot-eight sleaze, looked over when we stopped next to him, and I saw defiance cross his face and his chin lift. Harry urged the would-be buyer off a few feet and talked low, in Spanish, and gestured and jerked a thumb at the premises. The guy said, "Si, si. Gracias." and walked away fast.

Salter threw out his arms and said, "Aw, shit, Parker. Mind your own business, huh?"

I said, "He is. We are. We both are."

"What business? You wanna buy a car?" He grinned.

Harry stuck his hands in the pockets of his hoodie and said, "Got a message for you."

He loved doing that Chicago thing.

"Yeah? Who from?"

I said, "Me."

He looked disgusted. "I suppose it's about that Russell bitch."

I put a strong rein on my temper and said, "If you're hoping for a long life, Barry, you should stay away from Clare Russell."

Harry said, "How about a little demo?"

He reached out and slapped Barry smartly on one cheek and then the other. Harry stepped back and I took hold of Barry's wrist and twisted his arm behind him, jerked his hand up over his shoulder blade. He yelped. Harry slapped him again.

I said, "Do we do this again, Barry, or do you think you get it?"

He said breathlessly, "I get it. Really."

Harry said, "What a pussy."

I pushed Barry away and let go of his arm, and he staggered a couple of steps. I knew that bringing the shoulder muscles back to normal was almost as painful as the twist. Sweat was standing out on his face.

"Stay away," I said.

We turned and went back to Harry's car.

I said, "You see? An opportunity will usually present itself."

4

At six-twenty she came in the side door at Vincent's and walked down the aisle between the bar and the booths. She was all in black—pants, boots, man-tailored shirt, and long belted raincoat. I was in the fourth booth, on the inside, with a blondie named Nancy, who I used to fuck occasionally. There was an empty Pilsner Urquell bottle in front of me and a stemmed cocktail glass in front of Nancy. Clare stopped and I motioned for her to join us.

I said, "You look like a gun slick in that Henry Fonda movie."

She grinned and said, "Hi, Nancy," and slid in. The waiter stopped and she ordered a Bell's. I ordered another beer for myself and another Margarita for Nancy. I waved in the general direction of the back of the bar and a few seconds later Harry was with us. He said, "Shove over," and Clare did and Harry slid in next to her and set his beer glass on the table.

Harry grinned at Clare. "I thought you'd at least get your picture in the paper."

"What for?" Nancy asked.

He said, "Discovering the body."

"Whose body?" Nancy asked.

Clare said, "I didn't discover it, Sam did."

Harry said, "Well, I'm sure he'll let you discover the next one."

Nancy nudged me. "What body?"

Clare said, "No, that's okay. Discovering bodies is men's work."

Nancy said, "Where was it?"

"In Clare's front hall," Harry said.

Nancy's voice went up with excitement. "Really? Whose was it?"

Harry said, "An interesting question. Who *does* own a body?"

The waiter came and I paid and reached across to pour Clare's beer into her glass.

I said, "Gordy Terrell."

Nancy said, "I *know* him! Well, I mean, I know who he is!"

"Was," I said.

"Doesn't he come here sometimes?" She looked around.

"Did," I said. "Ever go to a party with him?"

"No, I don't think so. Why?"

"He took girls to parties."

Nancy made a face.

"Are we going to eat?" I asked.

"Oh, not me," said Clare. She gulped down half her glass of beer. "I have some things to do."

She shooed Harry out of her way, slid quickly out of the booth, and made for the front door of the bar.

Harry sat back down and said, "You are such a jerk."

I said, "Yeah," and tried to get up, but Nancy didn't move, just laughed. I said, "Let me out," and she laughed up at me.

I said, "Nancy, if you don't get the fuck out of my way, I will put you on the floor."

She laughed some more and I pushed her off the end of the bench onto the floor. She shrieked out a compound word no blondie should use in public. I stepped over her and followed Clare.

Behind me I heard Harry say, "They never believe him."

Her car was on the side street and I caught up with her just as she got her hand on the driver's door. I said, "Clare, wait. Hang on."

We stood facing each other in a thin, stinging rain that was wetting her face and flattening her curls.

I gave her my handkerchief and said, "What the hell was that about? You were going to eat with me."

"I wasn't—" Her voice broke and she started again. "I wasn't going to eat with *her*."

I said, "Can you drive?"

"Yes."

She dug into her pocket, extracted her keys, and then missed the door lock three times.

I reached over, took the keys from her hand, and said, "Come on, trade places," and walked her around to the passenger's side.

I started the engine and drove slowly out into the traffic. Her clenched left hand was on her left knee and I put my right hand around it, opened her fingers, and put my palm against hers. Her hand was icy.

She started to cry, turning her face away, hiding behind her other hand.

I drove into the empty parking lot of a bank, turned off the engine, and sat watching her for a second, then reached over and began to massage the back of her neck. She tilted her head forward a bit.

"Why are you crying?"

"I don't know."

"You just cry?"

"I'm tired."

"Tired."

"And I'm hungry. I didn't have any lunch."

"Right. Hungry."

She was quiet.

"That's it?" I asked.

She sighed. "Yes."

I put my hand with fingers spread on the top of her head. "All right, we'll go eat at Shueng's and then we'll go to your place and I'll leave you there and take your car and after the game I'll bring it back and everything will be fine. But no more crying."

She sniffled. "Okay."

5

Two hours later I parked her car across from her house. The rainy night seemed exceptionally dark when I cut the lights. I felt her hesitation.

"You going to be okay here for a few hours?" I asked.

"Of course."

"It's perfectly normal if you feel uneasy about being here. Not that I think there's any chance that anyone will back, but—"

"It's okay, really."

I said, "I could take you to a hotel. Or to my sister's."

"I'll be fine." She opened the door, swung her legs out, and stopped. "Are you coming in?"

"Absolutely." I opened my door. "You're sure about the hotel?"

"It's an interesting offer, but not tonight."

Upstairs she watched me check doors and windows and look in all the rooms, even in the closets and behind the shower curtain.

"You're being silly," she said.

"Does it make you feel better?"

A little defiantly, she said, "Yes."

"Me, too. I rest my case."

I had to stop saying that. It was something I'd picked up in L.A., like a bad cold.

She asked, "Will I see you later?"

"Doubt it. It'll be very late. Or very early. I'll just crash on your couch again. I still have a key, unless you changed the locks."

She nodded, then shook her head. "No. I didn't. You do. Sure."

I put my arms around her very gently, kissed her cheek, lightly, carefully, then jerked away from her, backed away, threw my arms out, turned and stomped across the room to the door to the hall.

"This isn't fair, you know," I said loudly as I jerked it open. I think I was talking to God.

"L.A. made you crazy," she said.

"I guess it did."

I went out, then looked back and said, "I'll come to thee by moonlight, though hell should bar the way. Lock this door behind me." She laughed and I pulled the door shut and after a moment I rattled the knob from the other side. "Clare, lock the door!"

I heard the deadbolt shoot home.

6

Harry and I both showed up at Kelly's still in our cool-weather garb. The Chicago big dog said, "Who brought the shit-kickers?"

So we kicked his shit.

WEDNESDAY, SEPTEMBER 14

1

When she came out of the bedroom in the morning I'd already made coffee and brought in the newspaper. We stood together in the kitchen, reading and drinking.

Finally I pushed myself away from the counter I was leaning against. I said, "I'm going to my sister's, then off to hustle."

I had a room, where Clare had never been, at Catherine's, who Clare had never met, where I kept my clothes and other belongings and which accounted for what little stability I owned up to. What I did for money—"hustling"—she pretended was maybe on another planet and not in English.

Actually, after Catherine's to shower and change, I was going to the office.

"His obituary's in the paper," she said abruptly.

"Whose, Gordy's?"

"Yes. The funeral's today. This afternoon."

"Let me see."

I read it quickly and shook my head. "Makes him sound almost respectable." I handed the paper back to her and watched her for a couple of minutes while she read the letters to the editor. She looked up and saw me watching her and blushed pink.

2

Cops, I'd read, go to victims' funerals. To see if someone looks too happy? Or guilty? I decided to go to Gordy Terrell's to see if there was anyone I knew. It was at a Roman Catholic church in the far reaches of the southern suburbs. The church was so far out that it was really in the country, and the graveyard was next to it. An old brick and stone church, with a newish brick addition in the back. Quite ugly. And who do I see dawdling in the parking lot? Clare, wearing her black raincoat. So I dawdled, too.

She didn't see me, though at one point I had to step behind the florist's van. I was driving Andy's car, which was a twelve-year-old dark green Honda. I didn't think she'd recognize it and I'd been making sure to arrive a bit late, to come in after they'd already begun. She sat near the back of the church, and I sat even further back.

I didn't participate. I figured one church is enough for any man and Greek Orthodox is plenty of church for me. In front of me Clare sat rigid, unmoving, also not participating, even though RC was the church of her childhood.

The mass ended and we all stood and the coffin was wheeled down the aisle to the door. The priest and the altar boys followed. The people in the front of the church rose and turned and followed—a couple in their sixties, a man in his thirties, and two children not quite teenagers. None of them looked much like the dead man. And none of them seemed to be weeping. The older couple looked tired and sort of baffled, and the younger man looked angry. The kids looked embarrassed. Maybe they were teenagers. The rest of the people in the church—not very many of them—came down the aisle after the family.

One was Denny Linden. He was there with another man, probably another cop. He was the last person to leave the pews, standing and watching everyone go by, taking everyone's attention from Clare, and me, as they shuffled out, giving him furtive looks. Then Linden and his pal turned and looked at Clare and me. When she turned to leave the pew, she saw me. I held out my hand and she came and took it and we went out.

Linden caught up with us on the steps and we four out-of-towners stood and watched everyone else watch the coffin go into the hearse for the short trip to the vehicle gate at the far side of the graveyard. Then everyone else started walking up the hill.

"You said you didn't know him," Linden said to Clare.

"I didn't."

"Why'd you come?"

"He died in my front hall." She shrugged. I still had her hand. "It just seemed like I should." She looked up at me, squinting against the glare of the overcast sky, then asked Linden, "Do you know who all these people are? Are they all from here? Are any of them from his—life?"

I was looking at them, a straggling line spread out through the graveyard, moving between the weathered headstones closer to the church to the newer section further away. It was starting to rain again, very lightly, and a few umbrellas popped up.

"I think they're probably all local," Linden said. "They don't look familiar." He turned a questioning expression on the other cop, who shook his head.

We all started toward the parked cars. We reached Clare's first and she unlocked the door, then turned back to Linden. "Do you know why he was killed?"

"Guys like him get killed." He walked away and his pal followed.

Clare looked after the last of the mourners going to the graveyard. She said, "They don't look like gangsters."

I said, "No, I don't suppose they would."

She looked more like a gangster's girlfriend than any of them did.

She stared out over the countryside. "I haven't been to mass since—I don't know. High school."

"You didn't take part."

"No. Someone inside me wanted to. I think it's bone-deep after parochial school. But I refused."

Why Clare's front hall? It nagged at me. She didn't know Gordy Terrell. Although Gordy Terrell probably knew who Clare was.

The killing looked almost as much like an attack on Clare as on Gordy Terrell. But why Clare?

SATURDAY, SEPTEMBER 17

We were at Bron's, having some late after-dinner drinks to celebrate my birthday, which was the next day. She had given me a matted and framed photograph of Harry, taken in a booth at Vincent's, face-on, that devil grin, just the way I'd see him so often over the card table. How did she know that?

"Why *my* house?" she asked me. "Why *my* front hallway?"

"Don't know, darlin'."

Bron's was as quiet as it always was, with cool piano music playing.

I said, "The only thing I can think of is someone wanted to get to me through you and didn't know I wasn't in town."

"Maybe I offended someone."

"What, you used the wrong fork?"

"Maybe I'm not a nice person after all. You don't know everything about me."

I laughed. "Dance with me," I said.

We went to a cleared space near the juke box and I put my arms around her and we began to move. This was new for us, the dancing. She was a good dancer, though a bit stiff.

"Who taught you to dance?" I asked.

"Harry."

I might have known. I pulled her a little closer.

"Have you found out anything?" she asked. "You were going to ask around."

"I did, a little, but no one seems to know anything. Not, you understand—" I whirled her around. "—that I have my finger on the pulse of the underworld—"

She said, "Of course not."

"—but I do know a few guys who are, shall we say—"

"Pulsating?"

"Exactly," I said.

"There," she intoned, "in the throbbing underbelly of the great metropolis—"

"Christ."

She said, "Well, I don't get the feeling you're taking this very seriously."

"The only part I'm taking seriously is that it was your front hall. Gordy Terrell was a creep. We're better off without him."

"Who's we?"

"The body politic."

Friday, November 18

So September and October went and most of November. I stayed in St. Paul, telling my family I was on vacation from traveling. They smiled. They knew exactly what I was doing there. Clare and I went to Vincent's for suppers and beers. Sometimes we went to Bron's. We ate Chinese and Mexican and Vietnamese and Thai. Twice I took her out to dinner at restaurants with white tablecloths and candles and dance bands that played swing music from the thirties and she became breathless dancing. We both liked dancing the lindy, but we also danced the waltz and the foxtrot and even the tango. A rather subdued tango, during which she laughed a lot and I was stern.

"You're an awfully good dancer," she said. "Much better than I am."

I said, "You're very good. You just need to relax a little. Maybe you'll feel easier when you get more used to me."

"Used to you?"

"I mean dancing with me."

"Are we going to do this a lot then?"

I said, "Yes. We are."

I pretty much forgot about Gordy Terrell and I think she did, too. And as far as I knew, Barry Salter was staying away.

I tried to sleep on her couch one or two or three nights a week without being too pushy.

One night in November we were in Vincent's, sitting across a table from Harry and his latest girlie. Not the tree girl. This girl was telling the ancient joke about the famous psychology professor and the student who knitted, and though Clare had heard it before, she'd had three beers and the girlie had a very funny way of telling it and Clare giggled until she had to turn and lean her forehead on my shoulder. Then she hiccupped and I pounded her on the back and she looked up and I looked back and smiled, and I guess that was when she first saw it in my face, that I was courting her.

What I saw in hers was wariness. *Do you mean it?*

We looked at each other.

And across the table Harry laughed and said, "By George."

But when we got back to her place, she was gone again. She tossed the comforter and pillow onto the couch and quickly shut the bedroom door behind herself. The next morning we drank coffee like no secret messages had ever been passed, and that afternoon I left town for three weeks in Houston and Miami.

SATURDAY, DECEMBER 24

1

By Christmas I was back in town. There was a heavy seasonal demand for portrait photography and Clare was working a lot. She photographed anybody and everybody, but she was becoming especially known for her pictures of children. On Christmas Eve I found her asleep in her desk chair. She woke up when I came in. I sat on the edge of the desk, and she yawned and tipped her head against my knee.

"What are you doing here?" she asked sleepily. "Why aren't you with your family?"

"I came to give you your Christmas present." I put it on her desk, a small foil-covered box, and said impatiently, "Open it."

She did and sat looking at it until I took it out of the box and laid it in her palm. It was a ring—a round, faceted, transparent blue stone set in a wide flat carved gold band. The band was somewhat worn.

"It's beautiful," she said.

"It's a sapphire."

She looked at me.

"Do you like it?" I asked.

"Like? I can't just *like* it. I'm *awed* by it. I don't know what to say. Are you sure you want to give it to me?"

"It's the color of your eyes. And it's your birthstone. Sometimes God does nice little coincidences like that. Put it on." I'd decided not to tell her I'd won it in a game. But I'd had it cleaned and appraised by the jeweler our family generally patronized.

"Is it old?"

"The jeweler said about a hundred years. Maybe more."

It fit her perfectly. I picked up her hand and admired it awhile.

She said, "My present for you isn't exactly wrapped. Well, it sort of is." She took a silky green drawstring bag the size of my thumb from a shelf by her desk and gave it to me. I felt something small and hard inside the bag and emptied it onto my hand. It was a carving in greenish white stone, Chinese, a smiling fat-bellied man with his arms stretched over his head.

I asked, "Is this jade?"

"The kind called nephrite. I got it from a jeweler I've known for several years and he assures me it's a good stone. It's a god named Ho Toy," she said. "He's the god of happiness and if you rub his belly he'll bring you good luck."

I said, "He's great. You can never have too much good luck."

2

Later we shared a beer in her kitchen. I said, "Come to my sister's to-morrow. Christmas dinner. All the trimmings."

She shook her head and opened her mouth, but I held up a hand to stop her.

"You don't do Christmas and you don't do families. You told me that. I didn't forget. I just hoped maybe you could change your mind. Just this once."

I busied myself lighting a cigar and swallowing the anger and didn't say anything more.

She looked away from me. "I decided a long time ago to give up Christmas. And all the trimmings. Not that I ever had it. I never did. Not even… when I was small. I don't know why."

I said, "What are you going to do?"

"Sleep late. Then I'll probably go to the Cochrans. They've invited me for supper."

Her professor and his wife.

"Good. At least you'll be fed." I levered my shoulders off the refrigerator and put the empty bottle on the counter. "I have to go."

Her face was carefully blank. She took a deep, slightly uneven breath. She was looking at the dark window. "What are you doing New Year's Eve?"

I said, "I was going to ask you to spend it with me, but I can't."

"You can't?"

"I'm working at a party."

"Working?"

"What're you, a parrot? My brother set it up. A casino party he's arranging for some people with more money than they need. What did you have in mind?"

"A party." She shrugged. "No one you know. I don't know them very well either. Clients."

I said, "Shall we have a date on Friday, eat dinner someplace? I'll buy."

"Sure. I'd like that. Thank you for the ring." She held out her hand, admired it. "It's the most beautiful thing I've ever had."

"You're welcome," and I gave her a quick kiss on the cheek. "Tell me Merry Christmas."

She put her hand on my wrist. She said, "*Kala Christougena.*"

I said, "Wow."

"Did I say it right?"

"Close enough. I recognized it."

"I googled it. I hope it's the right thing to say."

"Absolutely it is."

She shut the door behind me while I was still standing on the top step, looking back at her, like I always did.

Friday, December 30

"That detective, Linden. He came to see me."

"What for?"

"To ask me if I go to parties with you. I said sometimes we go to the same party. He said, together? I said sometimes."

"*Malaka.*"

"What's that?"

"Wanker."

She looked a little pink.

She said, "He said not your University-type friends—politics and art—that sort of thing. Parties with people Sam takes a lot of money from. Business types. Card games. Maybe a bunch of rich guys spending their money on some women. I said I don't know anything about that."

"You don't."

It was not a question.

"He asked me if I ever went to a party with Gordy Terrell. I told him I never saw that Terrell until he was dead. No and no, I said. I said I never went anywhere with Gordy Terrell, I never saw him until he was dead, and I don't think I ever went to that kind of party at all, not with anyone."

"That about covers it. Can I have your roll?"

"Yes. Then he said, you went to his funeral."

"And did you say so what?"

"I just said yes, you know I did, you saw me."

"You don't have to talk to him."

"I know. Then, he was leaving, and he said, he's not here and I don't have a witness, and if you want to tell me something you'd rather he didn't know, or that you'd rather he didn't know you told me, well—"

"He knows a lot of pronouns."

She shook her head. "As my mother used to say, Jesus Mary Joseph. Not an epithet of reverence. My God, I haven't thought about my mother for a long time."

When I walked her upstairs to her apartment and she was fumbling for her door key, I slid in between her and the door and put my hands on her shoulders and she looked up.

I said, "I'd like to kiss you. New Year and all."

She said, "Oh. Well. Would I like that, do you think?"

Did she just bat her eyes at me?

I said, "I'm a very good kisser."

"I *think* I would like it."

I pulled her forward a few inches and bent my head. Her lips were warm and a little rough. I'd buy her a crate of lip balm if she'd let me kiss her some more. I pulled away and she took in air.

She said, "You *are* good."

"Did you like it?"

"Why, yes. I did. Did you?"

I smiled. Oh, baby. I said, "Yeah, I did too." I stepped away from her. Very reluctantly. Harry and I had a date to play cards.

She found her key and opened her door and went in.

SATURDAY, DECEMBER 31

1

The casino party was given by some people named Jenneky. They owned a huge grotesquely modern house overlooking the river, yards and yards of glass and jutting roofs at odd angles. I was following Grant Jenneky into the card room when I saw Clare come in. I had already admired the collection of Jenneky portrait photos on the walls of the enormous entry hall and said aha! to myself.

She was all in black, her favorite look—wool cape, kid gloves, sheer black stockings, high-heeled black shoes with a bunch of straps. I think she believed that black made her look inconspicuous. Right. I wondered how she made it to and from her car in footwear like that.

I could see that she was scared, but I wasn't sure anyone else would see it; she looked very calm, very in control. It was in the clenched jaw and the mouth pressed closed. She was wearing makeup, not her usual style, and when Maggie Jenneky took Clare's cape, I saw three other guys turn their heads to look. Her dress had little thin straps and was made of shifting layers of filmy black stuff. My money said it was from the vintage store. She liked to shop there.

But she also liked to shop at a store that sold men's work clothes and at the Army-Navy surplus store and several thrift stores, and she made my heart jump and my breath go short when she showed up in khaki cargo shorts and a black T-shirt as much as she did in filmy black layers.

The only jewelry she was wearing were the Christmas ring and some little gold hoop earrings I'd sent her from L.A. for her birthday.

Maggie handed off the cape to a maid, who took it to a little cloak-room. Maggie was wearing a beaded and fringed white satin tube, very short, and carrying an ivory cigarette holder, and she had all the aplomb she needed to carry it off. She pulled Clare over to a group of guests, introduced her, pointed to the photographs, made sure Clare had a glass of Champagne, and went to greet the next arriving guest.

Grant touched my elbow and I went into the card room.

An hour later I took a break. She was watching six very excited play-ers at the roulette wheel when I came up behind her. Philip was across the table, acting as croupier. It didn't seem they'd gotten acquainted. She must have known just from looking at him that he was my brother. And he must have guessed who she was. Yet there they stood.

"What are you doing here?" I asked her softly.

She turned around. "I was invited by Maggie. She's a client."

I nodded. "Yeah, I saw the pictures. Having fun?"

"The only things I recognize are the slot machines and this." She gestured at the wheel. "And a bunch of people playing bingo. But it is fun. I saw you playing cards."

"That's the working part."

"You look very good at it."

"Yeah, I am."

She nodded. "You have a lot of chips."

"I do, don't I."

I put out my hand, palm up, and Philip set a roulette chip into it. I put the chip on the black diamond. He held his hand over the wheel and said, "No more bets," and spun it. She watched, fascinated. It came up black and I picked up my winnings, put them in her hands. Still speaking low, into her ear, I said, "See the croupier? Slim, dapper, good-looking? Looks like me? He's telling me to get back to work." I walked away while she and Philip looked at each other. I heard Philip say, "How do you do, Miss Russell. I'm Philip Zandros."

2

The next time I went looking for her, she was in the room that Maggie ingenuously—and she was about as ingenuous as Genghis Khan—called the picture room, and she was coming out, at full speed. A stockbroker protégé of Grant Jenneky's named Bobby Graff was right behind her.

She ran straight into me. I took her arms to steady her and said, "What's wrong?"

"Nothing. Really. Too much Champagne." She was shaking her head.

Graff came up behind her. "Fuck off," he said to me, and he put his hand around Clare's arm. "She's with me."

She tried to pull away but he kept hold of her. "Let go of me," she demanded.

I said to Graff, "Not any more. Hands off."

"What the hell, Zandros. You're out of line."

"Sam—"

Graff tried to pull her toward him, but I disengaged him from her arm by holding his thumb and bending it backward. He let go before the joint did.

He said, "*Fuck!*"

I said, "Hands *off*, Bobby."

Clare said in a hoarse whisper, "Damn it, Sam—"

We were both ignoring her but a number of people nearby were interested. Then Philip was between Graff and me, pushing us apart. He put a forearm in front of Graff and looked hard at me.

"Back off," he said. "Take her home and come back."

I made a snorting sound, said yeah to Philip, found Clare's hand with mine, and more or less pulled her away. We rounded a corner and I pulled her over to the wall and faced her.

"My brother is a bit old-fashioned sometimes. Do you *want* to go home? I'd be happy to stay and knock Bobby Graff on his butt."

"I do want to go home, but you don't need to—"

"Yes, I do. Wait here." I went into the cloakroom by the front door and came back with her cape. "Give me your keys. I'll bring the car up. Where is it?"

"I'll come with you. I don't want to stay here."

We went down the icy drive. I kept my arm firmly around her. I said, "How the hell do you walk in those things?"

"It's genetic," she said. "Why aren't you wearing a coat?"

"It's a guy thing. Here. Give me the keys."

"I can drive."

"No, you can't." I opened the door, helped her in, and went around to the driver's side.

"You've been drinking, too."

"You and several other people *think* I've been drinking. It's all an illusion." I started the engine, let it idle. "What happened in there?"

"He put his arm around me. And put his hand on me."

"That's it?" I raised an eyebrow at her. "You're too upset. He did more than that."

"He pulled my dress up and put his hand—in my panties."

"His mother is a whore. Okay. Don't worry about him. I'll deal with him later."

"He said, right out, he said that he would bring me business if I were nice to him. And he held my hand and wouldn't let go. Until I said I would scream!"

I smiled slightly and moved the car out into the road.

She said, "You were going to fight him."

"Not exactly. Knock him down, maybe. He wouldn't be interested in much more than that." I reached over and squeezed her wrist. I said again, "Don't worry about him."

She said, "You make all your money that way, don't you? Playing cards?"

"Yeah. You knew that."

She sighed. "Yes. I did, but—is it a lot?"

"Yes, it is."

"I didn't know it was a lot. Do you lose?"

"Sometimes."

She said, "Your brothers—make the arrangements?"

"Sometimes."

She said, "People want to play with you?"

"Uh huh."

"Because you're so good. And they want to win from you."

I said, "The better you are, the more money there is."

"Do you cheat?"

I laughed. "Honesty is the best policy, you know. No, I don't."

"Because if they found out, they wouldn't play with you anymore."

"And they might beat me up. Plus, I still like looking at myself in the mirror in the morning."

She said, "Do your brothers do that, too? Play cards?"

"Only as a sideline. We—the family—we have an office downtown. They make book. Take bets."

Her voice went up a key. "Like bookies?"

"Exactly like."

She shifted in the seat, turning to look at me. "Isn't that, well, dangerous?"

"It's just a business."

"I met your brother Philip."

I smiled. "The first one in the family to meet you. He'll be a very local celebrity."

"We didn't get to talk. He had to go settle a dispute in the bingo parlor." She put a hand out toward my arm and brought it back without touching. "You look so different tonight."

"You haven't seen me in uniform before."

"Is that what that is?"

"If I want to get a job as a headwaiter, I'm set."

"Yours looks a bit pricier than a headwaiter's. More class."

"You look pretty classy yourself, lady."

"Why, thank you. You're very nice for a headwaiter."

Ten minutes later I parked the car in front of her house.

She said, "I don't like all that money after all."

"I have to go back," I said. "I'll take your car and bring it back when I'm done." I opened my door.

"You don't need to come up."

"Yes, I do."

I kept my arm around her across the icy street and up onto the porch. When we entered her living room, I stopped her from turning on the ceiling light, and slid her cloak off her shoulders. "You are incredibly lovely tonight, Clare. Can I have my midnight kiss now?"

She turned and put her hands on my shoulders and kissed me sweetly. Wearing heels, she didn't really have to go up on her toes, but she did. I liked that. Then she whirled away and threw out one arm in a grand gesture. "Tonight I was Frances Russell. I was there because of my work. I was somebody. Because of my *work*."

"When aren't you somebody?"

"Never mind. Go."

"You did have some Champagne, didn't you?"

She kicked off her shoes, tripped over them, and threw herself onto the couch. "Yes I did. Here's the picture: Frances Russell drinks Champagne!"

I turned on a lamp and she blinked in the sudden glare.

"I confess," she said.

"Shouldn't you go to bed?"

"No. I want to be Frances Russell for a while longer." She slid over sideways to rest her head on the arm of the couch.

I lifted her feet up onto the cushion. There was a throw over the back of the couch, and I flipped it down to cover her. Car horns and cow bells sounded faintly through the closed windows.

I said, "Happy New Year, Frances Russell."

"Happy New Year, Sam," she said. Her eyes were closed. "Bye."

2012
SUNDAY, JANUARY 1

1

I came back at ten and found her on the couch again, this time sitting cross-legged, wearing red and white striped flannel pajamas and drinking tea.

"I think I preferred the dress, Frances Clare, but it's a hard call. Even money."

"Frances is hanging in the closet. It's just me, Clare."

"Clare's enough. Plenty. You look a bit wan. Are you hung over?"

"Wan? Have you been reading Jane Austen again? No, I didn't drink enough Champagne to be hung over. Maybe it's the stripes. Why do *you* look so good? You must have had a lot less sleep than I did."

"I'm used to it. Is there coffee?"

"If you make some. I'm drinking tea." She got up and followed me into the kitchen. "Did you know that what you do for a living is illegal?"

I smiled. "It is and it isn't. Not the poker. The games I play in, we're very careful not to do any of the things that make it look like it's being run by someone professional. Just a bunch of the guys in a friendly game." I measured coffee. "The bookmaking is something else. It's a felony. Does that bother you?"

"I don't know." She put her tea cup in the sink. "I think it should, but I don't know if it does."

I said, "Probably your association with me is destroying all your moral fiber."

She said, "Probably. And the few fibers I have left are dangerously deteriorated. You're shaved and everything. How long did you play cards?"

"About six."

"Then what did you do?"

Well, in for a penny, in for all the money in the world.

I said, "You're unusually inquisitive this morning." I gave her five seconds to change her mind. Then, "I drank two very expensive Scotch whiskies with Grant Jenneky and three of his friends and then, by invitation, I accompanied a very expensive young woman to her apartment downtown where I removed most of her clothing and some of mine and got my ashes hauled in her front hall. Then I—no, stay here—then I went to my sister's and cleaned up and changed clothes and came here to return your car and see you."

She was refusing to look at me.

I abandoned the coffee-making.

"Listen. Clare. Listen. Look." I was having trouble breathing. She looked. "Do you love me?" She blinked at me and opened her mouth. "Wait." She closed her mouth. "Damn! No, forget it, don't answer. Will you go to bed with me? Make love?"

"You already—" Her voice was harsh.

Mine was harsher. "I scratched an itch."

"Is this an itch?"

"No!" I pulled myself together. "It's a... a longing. An enduring desire."

"You're my friend."

"Christ! I know that. I think I want to be something else. More."

"I know," she said. She was keeping her eyes on the front of my shirt. "I figured that out. But—I don't know what you are any more. I don't know *who* you are. Are you my friend? Still? Maybe I don't know you." She was starting to sound a little frantic.

"Don't worry. I know you." I reached for her, put my hands on her shoulders.

"This is confusing," she said.

"It'll be all right."

"I can see already that it won't be," she said. "You're making things *different*."

"Yeah. I am. Very different. But different can be just fine."

I moved my hands up to hold the sides of her head, my thumbs under her chin to tilt her face up, and I bent forward to put my mouth on hers and ran the tip of my tongue over her lips. I could taste the tea she'd been drinking. My right hand slid behind her head, into her hair, and I kissed her, then made tiny little licks around her mouth some more. "I don't want to stop," I said, maybe a little too roughly.

She said, "This isn't fair."

I said, "Will you stop complaining? Yes or no?"

It came in a whisper. "Yes."

"Praise God," I said, not entirely lightly.

"Are you sure this is a good idea?"

"Yeah, I'm sure. A very good idea."

I led her by the hand into the bedroom and pushed the door shut behind us. She walked to the side of the bed. She said, "In the movies, he carries her into the bedroom. And there are white doves." I grinned at her as I took off my boots and socks. She let the pajama pants drop to the floor. The top covered most of her bottom. I stripped off my sweater and threw it over a chair, then gave her a come-along gesture.

She pulled the pajama top off over her head and stood in her little panties, and I stood with my hands stopped in mid-air on their way to my shirt buttons.

"My God, Clare," I said hoarsely, looking at her.

She could barely speak. "You saw me in the bath."

I unbuttoned my shirt. "You were covered with bruises. It's not the same, believe me."

She watched me drop my shirt on top of the sweater and unbutton my jeans, and put her palm ever so lightly on my chest. I shivered. Jesus, I was going to come right there.

I stepped back, kicked off my jeans and shorts, pulled back the covers on her bed, and sat down and pushed her panties down to her feet.

"This isn't very romantic," she said.

"Later." I moved across the bed, pulling her after me. I wanted to be gentle but that wasn't going to happen. "Oh, God. I knew you would feel like this. Jesus. I can't wait, Clare." I rolled on top of her and pushed carefully into her—she said *aaah* deep in her throat.

She surprised me again. No holding back. No hesitation. Total participation. Except for one ever-so-brief moment early on when she went all still and I said in a low voice, "Don't worry, it's okay," and then she was soft again.

I was totally absorbed, by the sex, by her. When we were done, she lay limp and wet and trembling under me.

"Oh, Sam," she whispered, and again, "Oh, Sam."

"Liked that, did you?" I croaked.

"Oh, yes." She turned her head to kiss me and said it again, into my mouth. "Yes yes yes." She kissed me several more times.

When I had more breath, I asked, "Do you always make that noise when you come?"

"What noise?"

"You growled. I thought for a second I was hurting you."

"No, you didn't hurt me."

I lifted myself onto my elbows, and looked down at her face.

She said, "You're awfully good at this."

"I've been watching you, thinking about how to take care of you."

"We fit together." She ran her hands down my naked butt.

I said, "Yin and yang."

"Have I lost a friend?"

"We'll figure something out."

She fell asleep, and I pulled the covers over her. Over us. I dozed, then woke up and woke her, and we made love again.

"For the rest of the day," I said when we were done, "I'll be watching football on a big-screen TV in a noisy bar. Will you come with me?"

"Sure. Can I do the crossword puzzle?"

"Yes." I started to sit up, but she put her hand on my arm.

"Can I bring the Nikon?"

"Yeah." I tried again to get up.

"Wait."

"Hurry, they're kicking off soon."

"I don't look like... all those others."

"Other whats?"

"Those women you go out with."

"No, you don't." I put my hand under her head and tilted it up. "Look at you. You look like a woman, for Christ's sake. Breasts, hips, nice round belly and bottom. A place to grow babies."

She was blushing. "But they're all beautiful. They all look like—"

"Racehorses."

She giggled.

"Clare, darling, they're glamorous, not beautiful. They spend a lot of money on themselves, and none on food. You look like a wonderful, healthy, jumpy little pony."

"A what?"

"A pony." I grinned. "My brother Philip, who you met last night, told my sister that you are the real thing."

"The real thing. He doesn't even know me."

"He knows me. Get dressed."

"When did he tell her that? Was she there? At the party?"

"No, he and his family came to breakfast."

2

We went to a seedy sports bar named Elmore's where several customers knew me but Clare knew no one and no one knew her. During the first game she drank two beers, ate popcorn, and read the newspaper and actually worked the crossword puzzle. Every now and then the long-lensed Nikon came up unobtrusively and she took one or five or ten shots. Though once I had to put a hand on her arm and say quietly, "Uh uh. Not him." He was a high-stakes player, not just cards. It was said he had some rather nasty habits.

At the end of the game I collected money from several men.

"How much did you win?" she asked me.

I shrugged. "Not much. Four-fifty."

"Four hundred and fifty dollars?"

"Yeah. Are you hungry?"

"Yes. And you're buying."

During the second game she nibbled her way through four slices of pizza, drank two more beers, and shot more pictures. I offered to explain the play to her.

"First explain to me why they do this," she said, "and why we care."

"Never mind," I said.

Shortly after the second game began, Harry came in and raised his eyebrows at Clare. "Jesus, what are you doing here? Ah. Something happened." He grinned happily. "Yes!" and gave me a sketch of a punch on the shoulder.

I grinned back at him.

"Louts," she said.

3

We drove back to Clare's in a snowstorm.

"Park in back," she said. "They might plow."

I drove down the alley and fitted the Honda into a space between two sets of trash containers. When I turned off the engine, she tucked both her hands around my arm and leaned her head against my shoulder.

"What is it?" I asked.

"Harry knew."

"Harry knows us both real well. And, of course, the mark of Cain on your forehead."

"And that money. How much?"

"Mmm, seven, seven-fifty."

"You really know exactly, don't you?"

"Pretty much. What's wrong?"

She shrugged. "I don't know. Things about you that I didn't know. A whole different world, another world that you live in that I didn't even know about, maybe more than one other world. And Champagne last night and not enough sleep and all that noise and beer—and pizza—and I'm going to have my period."

"God, I hope so."

"Mmm, yes."

"And you're afraid you lost your friend."

"Did I?"

I kissed the top of her head. "What do you think?"

"I don't know what to think! And I really am tired."

We sat in the warm car while the snow covered the windshield. She sighed and wiggled into a more comfortable position.

I couldn't think of what to say to her. "We'll figure something out," I said finally. Maybe I was tired, too.

She said, "You said that before."

"It might take more than one afternoon. Come on, Clare, I'm still the same man I was before I went to bed with you."

She said gloomily, "I don't think I'm the same woman."

"A lot of women react to me that way," I said. I pushed her up off my shoulder. "There's nothing to worry about. I made love to you and I liked making love to you and I plan to do a lot more of it."

"And that's what counts?" There was an edge in her voice.

I said, "Yes, it counts, but it's not *all* that counts. You know that much about me."

She sighed. "Yes. Yes, I know that much about you. Maybe I can learn the rest."

"Let's go in."

Monday, January 2

She came in the front door at Vincent's and stopped just inside to look for me. I looked up and saw her. For a moment, moisture sparkled on her hair and lashes and I felt myself stir.

Nancy, the blondie I'd tossed on the floor, inched closer to me. She was holding a drink in a stemmed glass and had been basking in being the focus of my attention. Clare walked over to us, stopping just out of reach as she saw my hand start to come out to her. I had my back to the bar, leaning on it, and I grinned at Clare and walked away from the blondie.

We found an empty booth in the back room and I put her coat and muffler—she still shopped at the military surplus—on a coat hook and sat next to her, shoving her over toward the wall, and put my arm around her and kissed her cheek and the corner of her mouth. "You look great," I said. "And you smell greater."

She was looking around the room. Several people we knew were looking back. "Why don't you just make a sign for the table?" she muttered.

I said, "They'll all know soon enough, anyway. Do we care?"

"You do. You love every minute of it."

I said, "Sit closer."

She leaned against me and laughed. Harry came in and sat in our booth.

We sat together and ate and drank and people came and went and talked about films and books and politics and other people. But tonight my ankle rubbed hers and my hand was on her arm or her back or her shoulder, and our friends and most of our acquaintances knew that it was different. Friends smiled, others were probably making predictions of disaster. Someone was no doubt making book. Nancy came through with a tall dark stranger and squinted at us as if we were someone she might recognize if she thought hard.

"Oh, fuck her!" Clare said loudly, and Harry grinned.

WEDNESDAY, JANUARY 4

1

Harry and I were playing in a game in an expensive downtown condo. There was plenty of booze, but I was doing my tasting act and he was drinking fizzy water with a lemon slice in it. We were both getting good cards and playing smart and taking a lot of money.

"What time you quitting?" I asked him while someone was being contemplative.

"Three."

"Can you give me a ride?"

"Sure."

We left on time with a lot of money from several sour-looking men.

"You hungry?" he asked.

"I could eat."

We stopped at the Hmong's.

Harry said, "So you got your brand on the little dogie."

"She's still somewhat skittish," I said.

"The cards? The wine, women, and song?"

"The cards, I guess. And the family for sure. And the whole brand thing."

"She looks tied up and delivered."

I said, "Yeah. But she's been on her own a long time. Even longer than you and I know about, I'm guessing. Not that she should have been on her own, she shouldn't, she was too young, but even so, I think she's having trouble giving that up."

2

She was asleep when I came in, but she woke up when I said her name softly and touched her shoulder.

"It's me."

"Uh huh." she muttered. "Iss you."

I sat down on the bed to take off my shoes and socks, then stood to shuck the rest of my clothes. "Wake up," I said as I got under the covers.

"I'm sleep."

"I know. Wake up. I passed on a blondie to get back here."

She sighed deeply. "More fool you. No blondies here." She turned over to face me. "But since you're here…"

THURSDAY, JANUARY 5

We threw on yesterday's clothes and walked out into the cold sunny morning for breakfast at Mr. Salmon's deli and superette on the corner. We sat at the counter and had coffee and fresh juice and bagels with cream cheese. I bought a paper, and we had finished eating and she had finished the news sections and the editorials and she was reading the feature section and I was reading the sports pages when I became aware that she was tapping her fingers on the counter. Without looking at her, I said, "Stop fidgeting. What is it?"

"Was there really a blonde?"

I looked up from the newspaper. "There's always a blonde if you look hard enough. What are you talking about?"

"You said that you passed on a blondie."

"Yeah, I did. It was the blondie or a ride home from Harry. I chose Harry." I paused for a few seconds. "Cards, liquor, women—it's a set."

"Are they prostitutes?"

"Yes, of course. Although some of them are close to being amateurs."

"And usually you would—" She waved a hand. "—partake?"

"I love your vocabulary. You know I would. Usually." I pushed the newspaper away. "We've talked about this before. As friends. You know me."

"I think I do."

I said, "So now we talk about it as lovers?"

Mr. Salmon behind the counter gave me a very hard look, then went back to stacking cups.

I said, "Okay. I won't be changing."

She nodded, very serious.

"Don't ask it, don't even think it. Don't think about it. It has nothing to do with you."

She shook her head, then nodded. "Okay."

Friday, January 6

Theophany. I stood in church with all my family, feeling the absence of Clare. If I did everything right, she could be here with me next year.

SATURDAY, JANUARY 21

Does a life have theme music? Those Were the Days, My Friend. What did we have? An affair? A liaison? It was new, smooth, glowing, full of promise. It was secret and passionate. Complete but never enough, never enough. She was glory to me. She said almost nothing about us, but her touches had destiny in them.

WEDNESDAY, JANUARY 25

We were having a quiet evening on her couch. She was sitting at one end reading catalogues and photography magazines, and I was stretched out with my head propped against her leg, watching a basketball game on television. Her landline phone rang and she waited for the machine to click on, then waited through her message, and then listened for the incoming message. When the caller's somewhat slurred voice came on I felt her stiffen.

"Hey, Clare, it's me, Barry. Why don't you ever answer your phone? I'll come roun' see you some day. Ol' time sake, and all that."

There was a beep as the connection was broken.

I twisted around and reached and very deliberately removed the phone cord from its socket, wanting to rip it out but knowing that would anger Clare and perhaps frighten her, and I didn't want to do that. I looked up at her face. She was already frightened.

"Is this the first time he's called?" I asked.

She pleated the corner of a catalogue. "Well, not exactly. He called me once, well, twice, in the middle of the night and said—things. And a couple of times there've been calls where nobody said anything. Hang-ups."

"Tomorrow you get an unlisted number."

"I can't do that. I have a business. I have a website. People call me."

"Okay, you use this number for business and never answer it. Just get messages, call people back. Nobody will think that's odd. They'll just think you're shooting. And unplug it at night. Use your cell for all your personal stuff. Does he have your cell number?"

"I don't think so. I keep that pretty private."

"If he keeps it up, let me know. I can dissuade him."

"He was just drunk."

"That makes it worse, not better." I sat up. "You think that if you ignore him, he'll go away, but he won't. You're wrong. Are you going to do as I say about the phones?"

"As you say? I've been taking care of myself since I was—for a long time—and suddenly it's as *you* say?"

I took a deep breath and let it out. "Clare, don't give me a speech. I know guys like Salter and I know you can't take care of yourself. Not like that. He's mean and you're not. He's determined to hurt you and you aren't determined not to be hurt."

"And I'm a dumb broad and you're not."

"Exactly."

I lay down on the couch again, adjusted my head, and fixed my eyes on the television screen.

After a few minutes she said, "All right. I'll take your advice about the phones." After another few minutes she said, "I didn't know you even liked basketball."

"I have a moderately significant bet down."

"How much is significant?"

"Five."

"Hundred? Dollars?"

"Uh huh."

Significant to her. I didn't often bet on sports, but it was some action on a quiet night.

She sighed.

Friday, January 27

I decided I would go ahead and dissuade Salter after all, but when I asked around a little, no one seemed to have seen him recently and I lost interest.

MONDAY, JANUARY 30

We'd made love. She was lying on her back and I was face down, my arm on top of her, my hand cupping her breast. I could feel her heart beating.

"Clare?"

"Mmm."

"What do you think about getting married?"

Her heart thudded and I grinned into the sheet.

She said quickly, "I think it's a really good idea for people who want to, but not so good for people who don't."

"Boy, you know how to go out on a limb."

"I believe in speaking my mind."

I said, "How do you stand on *being* married? To me, for instance."

She took a deep breath. "Is this a quiz? Should I be taking notes?"

I got up on my elbow. "I want to marry you. I want you to marry me. I want us to marry each other. Is that straight enough for you?"

"Is it a question or just an announcement?"

"Jesus Christ, Clare. It's a question, an interrogatory statement. Will you marry me?"

"I don't know."

Was she thinking about that lying Irish skunk O'Connell? We had never discussed him.

I said, "How can you not know?"

"Why make it different? Why make it different *again*?"

"I want you—"

"You've got me!"

"—and I want children." I moved my hand to her belly. "I want to put babies in there. Yours and mine. Ours."

Her breath caught in a sort of startled sobbing sound.

"Say yes, darling," I coaxed.

"I don't know," she whispered.

I leaned over and kissed her gently, and caressed her lips with my tongue.

"Don't do that! I'm trying to think. What about your family? They don't know me. I'm not Greek."

"They want to know you."

"And you don't know my family."

"What family? Be real. Your father's dead so long you don't remember him and you haven't seen or talked to your mother for, what, six years? Seven? Ten?"

"Shouldn't I tell her if I get married?"

"Send her a card. Come with me to my sister's, now, for dinner. She wants to meet you. They all do."

"All? How many are there?"

"My sister, my brothers and their wives—"

"How many brothers?"

"Just two. And their kids, and my Uncle Nick, and my cousin—"

She put her hand over my mouth. "I can't do that. Not yet. Later. Please."

"All right. But you'll think about it?"

"Yes, I promise. I'll think about it."

SUNDAY, FEBRUARY 6

I'm going to have a show," she said. She had been closing her phone when I came in. Her announcement was very low key, but I could see the excitement in her face, hear it in her voice.

"Wow. When? Where? Can I come?"

"No, it's only for adults. You know that new rehabbed warehouse place down in Lowertown that has about twenty art shops and galleries in it? And restaurants and bars?"

"Creekside Landing."

"Right. There's a gallery there called Hundred. Just opened. I went to the U with the owner, Ellie Bragg, and I was there last week. She's going to specialize in showing photography. She'll do a hundred photos at a time from just one photographer, for one or two weeks, maybe more. Mine will be all portraits. She wants me ready to open on March second. Part of a big neighborhood art crawl. That way there will be time to get a review into the Sunday paper. I'm going to meet with her tomorrow, to look at the space and work out the details."

She was starting to glow, and I grinned at her. "I guess an autograph is out of the question."

"See my agent." She went to her desk. "I have to make a list. I'll have to get permissions from everyone I want to put in the show!"

SUNDAY, FEBRUARY 20

I came in late and caught her hurriedly pushing a bundle of papers into a desk drawer. "What was that?" I asked as I dropped my jacket on a chair.

"Nothing."

I laughed. "You look like I just caught you with your paw in the fish bowl. What was that?"

"Just my bills." She rubbed her eyes.

"Why are you hiding them?"

I stood in the middle of the room looking down at her, and she gazed attentively at her own hands. Her answering tone was all airy innocence. "So I don't have to think about them and you won't see them because if you see them then we'll have to talk about them and then I'll have to think about them. Very simple, really."

"To you, maybe. All right, we'll skip the part where I see them and go straight to talking about them. Can I assume this means you haven't paid them?"

She folded her arms on the desk and put her head down on them. "Yes."

"Why not?"

"I can't." Her voice was muffled.

"Why not?"

"Not enough money."

"Why not?"

Her voice rose. "I'll take care of it after the show."

"After the show, huh. Are you really going to have some money then?"

"I've had some extra expenses lately."

"For the show."

"Yes."

"Why didn't you tell me?" I went into the kitchen and came back with two bottles of Summit. She liked the IPA, which was fine with me. So I kept her supplied. Unobtrusively. "Or ask me."

"I knew you'd say that."

"Oh, you did, did you?" I set the beers on the desk and stood behind her and began to massage her shoulders.

"Yes."

"So answer."

"Crawl up to you and say, please, kind sir, I can't make it on my own after all?" She sat up, stiff under my hands. "My work means nothing to you, does it? You just want a baby factory. Taking pictures is just something to fill up my time until I come to my senses and get married, like a real Greek girl would."

"Hey, Frances, if you want to start a fight, start a fair one." I dug my fingers in and felt her subside. "I never said or thought any of those things. I'm not the one in this room who's worried about how important your work is. I *know* how important it is. Which is very. And I'm not the one who seems to think that marriage and family are only for the artistically impaired."

"Shut up, shut up." She put her head down again. "I'm too tired to argue with you. And you always win."

"Yeah, think about that. So tomorrow you can do me a favor."

"What favor?" She lifted her head and drank some beer.

"Say you will."

"Before you tell me what it is? Just how dim do you think I am?" She twisted her head sideways and showed me a narrow-eyed look.

"Say you will."

"All right! If it doesn't take more than half an hour. I'm a busy woman."

"It will take no time at all. I will hand you a large sum of money and you will kiss me sweetly and say thank you, kind sir."

"That's a favor to you?"

"Let me pretend, for just a few fleeting moments, that I am taking care of you."

She laughed. "Just when did you get off that boat from Athens? Okay, I can't resist you. I'm too tired and too worried. I'll pay you back after the show." Two beats. "Do I really have to say 'kind sir'?"

"Absolutely. That's the best part."

SATURDAY, FEBRUARY 25

1

When she woke up I said, "You know, young women, like you for instance, are not supposed to have big dark circles under their eyes. That consumptive look went out with the bustle."

"I'm fairly sure I'm not consumptive."

"You need some fresh air. Displace all those chemicals you've been breathing in for weeks. Let's go spend the afternoon by the river."

"I delivered the show photos to Ellie yesterday. I guess I could sneak in a free afternoon."

"Won't cost you a penny," I promised.

2

We had a favorite walk along the river. The park people kept the paths plowed all winter, and we could make a short loop or go for miles. The sun was out and it was starting to feel ever so slightly like spring, even with the snow still on the ground. She brought a little digital point-and-shoot that was about the size of a deck of cards, and she took some pictures of me that made me look twice and I took some of her that made her laugh. We walked about two miles downriver and then two miles back, and then, feeling full of virtue, went for Thai food before going back to her place. She opened the door to her apartment, switched on the light, and screamed. Not a big scream, not loud or long, but from her gut. I put her aside, not as gently as I could have, and walked in.

"Oh, shit," I said.

3

Everything I could see had been smashed, torn, or cut to ribbons.

"Go back down the stairs and stay there," I said. "I'm going to see if anyone's still here."

"No! Don't! There's no one here. I'd know. They say you shouldn't go in. I read that. Please, don't." She had a death grip on my sleeve.

"Just wait here. I don't think there's anyone, either, but I want to look."

"That's stupid, you know it is."

Her voice rose and she pulled harder on my sleeve and I knew she'd follow me if I went in unless I got rough. "Okay. Okay. We'll both go down."

She nodded and turned, started down, and stumbled, and caught herself on the railing.

I said, "Damn it, don't *fall* down."

She stopped and turned. Her teeth were chattering. She clenched them. "Will—will you call the police? I don't think I—can."

"Do you have insurance?"

"What?"

"Insurance. Do you have any? If you do, we call the cops."

She started down again. "Oh. Yes. On my—my cameras—" She turned and ran into me, tried to go past me. "My cameras. I have to see—"

I stopped her. "Uh uh. First we call the cops. Come on, we'll wait in the car."

The car was still warm, but she was shivering so hard I thought she might break a tooth. I got out of my jacket and tucked it around her lap, and then I called 911.

4

Two uniforms came first. They asked me if I'd been inside and I said no. So they went in and soon came out again. Clare stayed in the car and I stayed with her, standing outside the car. Just as they came out, an unmarked car arrived and Denny Linden got out. The uniforms nodded at him and said, "Sergeant."

"You get thrown out of Homicide?" I asked.

"It's Robbery-Homicide, and this is a burglary but it might be connected. Stay here." Linden drew out his gun and went into the house. The uniforms, guns drawn, followed. Then one of them came out onto the porch and motioned us in.

I stood where I could see her every minute, but mostly we all left her alone, to go from room to room, looking, not touching.

She had stopped shivering, but she looked horribly pale.

In the living room, cushions and upholstery were ripped open, books torn apart, computer and television and tape player smashed, and flour and ketchup and beer smeared into the rug.

She was not very interested in the kitchen, where shards of glass and broken china covered every surface, and pans and flatware were strewn about, and shelves of food and the contents of the refrigerator were dumped out on top of everything.

In her workroom, chemicals were spilled and prints torn and drawers of negatives dumped on the floor. The printers and enlarger were reduced to fragments and twisted metal.

She hesitated at the door to the bedroom and I moved to stand in the doorway after she went in. The futon mattress and pillows and sheets and duvet had been slit open and her clothes ripped and cut and torn to shreds. Someone had made a pile of her panties and bras and had urinated on them. The smell was strong in the closed room. The mirror was broken and her jewelry box twisted apart and empty. Even her chest of drawers was a wreck, and I finally realized that he'd used an axe as well as a knife.

She glanced into the bathroom: spilled cosmetics and more broken glass.

The door to the studio was ajar and she stood in front of it for a long minute before I reached around her to push it all the way open. Then she stepped into the wreckage of cameras and lights. The volume of debris was much less than in the other rooms, but she stood in it without moving for a long time.

Denny Linden made notes and asked questions and I answered them with my eyes on Clare. Linden was polite to Clare but it was me he watched.

"Is anything obvious missing?" Linden asked her.

She shook her head.

He looked at me. "Any idea who did this?"

"No," I said.

"Miss Russell? Any ideas?"

She shook her head again.

"Has anyone threatened you? Obscene phone calls? Anonymous letters? Anyone mad at you?"

She shook her head to all of it.

"Uh, Sergeant?" It was one of the patrol officers.

They'd found a body out by the alley. It was Barry Salter.

5

Linden herded us into a corner of the living room, out of the pathway from front door to back. I kept my arm around her. She was shivering again, staying upright on her own, but just barely. It had been almost two hours since we'd walked into the carnage.

"The victim is Barry Salter. You..." Linden made a small gesture at me, "...identify him and his ID backs it up. You both say you knew him."

I nodded. "Uh huh."

"How long?"

I shrugged. "Three years? Maybe longer."

"Same for you, Miss Russell?"

She looked blank, then looked at me. I just looked back. No prompting the witness. She cleared her throat. "Same what?"

He was patient. He was used to it. "How long did you know Barry Salter?"

"Oh. Two years? Something like that."

"How well did you know him?"

She pulled herself together. "We dated. For... a few weeks. Before that, not much. I mean I didn't know him much. He was—I'd see him. Around. But we had different friends. I didn't really know him."

Technicians going through the kitchen, to and from the back door, crunched over everything on the floor, until someone found her broom and pushed most of the debris aside, out of their path.

A police photographer came in and shot pictures of the vandalized rooms, and she watched with a strange look on her face.

"And then he asked you out?"

She nodded absently, watching the photographer.

Linden looked sideways at me. "Where were you?"

"L.A."

To Clare: "Did he take you to parties?"

"No." She shook her head and brought her attention back to Linden. "I don't much like parties."

"Where did he take you?"

"I went to the Film Society with him. And... out to eat. And he came here and watched TV. And then he—" She stopped.

Denny said, "He what?" But he and I both knew.

She said it very fast. "He slapped me and he pulled my hair."

The anger went through me like a flame but I kept it in. The bastard was already dead, and we no longer lived in a society that accepted mutilating corpses.

Denny said, "Tell me again when you left here today and when you came back."

I said, "We left about eleven. We got back at nine. Maybe a little after."

He flipped back in his notes. "Call came in at nine-eighteen."

A tech came in and looked at Clare's fingerprints with a magnifying glass, then at mine. Linden said he supposed my prints were on file and I said yeah.

"If you hear anything, you'll let me know," he said to me. It wasn't a question.

"Are you done? I want to get her out of here."

The techs locked up the back and then clattered down the front stairs with all their gear. The uniforms followed, then Denny. I locked the door behind all of us, took Clare's hand, led her across the hall and down the stairs.

Denny said, "Where will she be?"

"My sister's."

"Kamariotis."

I said yes, and we all went out to the street and to the cars and Linden watched us leave.

6

In the car she said, "The beer cans. There were some Saturday Special cans. I never drink it and I never saw you drink it. But Barry drinks it. He was *in* there—"

"He brought his own beer. The perfect guest." I'd pulled over to the curb and I was punching numbers into my phone. "I'll tell Catherine we're coming."

"Sam, I can't—"

"You will." I turned to face her. "Did you see what someone did to your clothes? Your panties and bras? And your bed? He used a knife, Clare, and then he used it on Salter. Can you think for even a second that I'll let him use it on you?"

She shivered.

Catherine answered.

"Sam. I'm bringing Clare. Her apartment was vandalized while we were out this afternoon and—there's more—I'll tell you when I get there. Listen, are the kids in bed? Good. She couldn't take them now. Who else is there? Okay, Philip and you, but no one else. Fifteen minutes."

Catherine lived in an older but very well-kept-up apartment building that she owned. She and her late husband Stephanios had moved into her building as newlyweds and she had always brushed off suggestions that she move. She'd taken over two other apartments and remodeled everything into a large comfortable space for her, the three kids, and, incidentally, me.

The lobby was warmly modern and manned by two armed security guards, one of whom took Clare's car keys from me. He would put the car into my reserved spot in the garage under the building. The other one had his hand on the intercom. He would call Catherine to tell her we were on our way up. The elevator lifted us smoothly to the fourth floor. The corridor lights were dimmed for the night.

Catherine stood in the open doorway at the end of the hall, Philip behind her. My sister was forty years old, a dark, intense woman, about Clare's size but curvier. I introduced them.

Catherine embraced Clare gently and warmly and Philip embraced her gently and formally and kissed her cheek. I helped her out of the long parka that she was still wearing from our afternoon walk, and dropped it with mine on a chair.

Catherine took Clare's hand and led her into the large warm comfortable living room. "I've made tea," she said. "Are you hungry? Did you eat?"

Clare gave me a panicked look and shook her head and I said, "No food. We ate. Tea's good." I sat her down on a long couch and sat beside her. "Something warm."

Catherine sat by a large tea tray and poured. "The guest room is all ready. It's very quiet."

Clare's hand groped for mine and I took it. It was like ice. "She'll stay in my room, with me."

Catherine handed a cup and saucer to Clare, and the cup clattered on the saucer as she took it. I helped her steady it. "Sugar?" Catherine asked. "Milk? Sugar would be good for you."

Through her clenched teeth, Clare said, "No, thank you."

"Brandy," said Philip.

Clare shook her head, and I said, "I'll take some."

Philip rose and went to the bar cabinet.

Clare sipped tea and wrapped her hands around the cup and relaxed a little.

"What happened?" Philip asked.

"I'll tell you later," I said. "How'd you do on the Wolves?"

"Very good." Philip put my drink on the coffee table, leaned back in his chair, and lit a small cigar. "We did good on all but the Lakers."

We talked sports results a while longer, until Clare was sagging against my arm and her teacup was in peril. "Come on, Frances Clare, time for bed." I took away her cup and pulled her to her feet. Catherine and Philip stood also.

I said, "I think I can handle this," and Philip grinned.

Catherine put her hand on Clare's arm. "Ask us for anything. Any time."

In my room I helped Clare to undress down to her panties and got one of my flannel pajama tops on her—I never used the tops—and tucked her under the covers of my bed.

There was a quiet knock on my door. It was Catherine. She didn't say anything, didn't come in, just put a hot-water bottle into my hands.

I sat down next to Clare and tucked the hot-water bottle in with her. She hugged it. I said, "I need to talk to Philip. I'll be in the apartment, I won't go anywhere. If you need me for anything, just yell or come and find me, okay?" She said yes with her lips but no sound came. "This is a very high-security building. You're completely safe here." She pulled a hand from under the covers and held it out. I squeezed it. "I won't be long. Go to sleep. I'll leave the desk light on."

"Thank you for letting me stay here," she said very seriously.

I said, "It seemed more convenient than a hotel." I saw her eyes go out of focus as I stood up.

Catherine had taken away the tea things and was in a large chair with a glass of red wine. Philip had refilled our brandy glasses and was in another large chair. They had turned on the TV but he clicked it off when I came back in. I took the couch again, leaned forward, forearms on knees, and picked up my glass. I was tired and starting to let down.

"Tell me what happened," Philip said.

"Everything she owned, gone. Smashed. Destroyed. All her cameras, lights, her darkroom, everything. Her clothes, dishes, books—"

Catherine said, "God in heaven."

I said, "It was unbelievable. So *cruel*. Her face—" I drank some brandy, leaned back, rested the glass on my thigh. "And a body on her back steps. Outside but, um, connected."

Catherine said, "Oh God!" and Philip said, "Who?"

"His name is Salter. *Was* Salter. A punk. Sells some drugs. I think he might be connected to Kevvy Smith. *Was* connected. Small time. She was seeing him, before I came back from L.A. I don't think she knew about the drugs, or about Kevvy. She told him to beat it."

"Did you help him out?"

"No." I sipped brandy. "I wish I'd had the chance. He manhandled her a bit. He's been calling her on the phone."

"What are you going to do?"

"Look for who was with him. Salter was in the apartment, we know that much." I told him about the beer cans. "He helped someone tear it up, then his buddy stuck a knife in him on their way out."

"Another knife."

"Yeah. Maybe the same knife."

"Do you know who?"

"No. Probably someone who knew both Gordy Terrell and Salter. That already narrows it down to a few hundred. But Salter's got a brother. Guess I'll ask him first."

"Don't look for him alone. Take Andy."

"I won't need any help."

"You will if he has friends. Don't be stupid. Take Andy. I insist."

"All right."

Philip took a tin of small cigars from his pocket, looked at it, and put it back. "Her father's dead."

"Right. She was five, doesn't remember him much, doesn't know anything about him except that he was Irish. Her mother, we assume, still lives in San Diego, but Clare hasn't had any contact with her since she was fifteen."

He stood up. "Call the office in the morning, tell me how she is."

Catherine and I watched him go, heard the door close. "He's tired," she said. "He worries about you. He wants you settled down."

"What the hell, I want me settled down. There's only one person left to convince." I poured more brandy. "I wish that when you saw her it wasn't just after she'd been bludgeoned like this."

"She's lovely, even shocked as she is."

"There's no other woman like her, anywhere."

She stood up. "I'm going to bed. I'll see to the doors."

I finished my brandy. Clare was asleep when I came to bed, but she woke me several times in the night, turning restlessly, talking in her sleep, once sitting up and saying my name and crying out no no no. Each time I held her and rubbed her back and talked softly into her ear until she relaxed and slipped back into sleep.

SUNDAY, FEBRUARY 26

1

I woke up before she did, and showered, dressed, went to the kitchen for coffee, managing to avoid the kids, and brought it back to my bedroom to drink. Her eyes were open when I came in, but they were focused on the ceiling and she lay inert under the cover. I sat on the side of the bed and ran the tip of a finger down her cheek.

I said, "How are you? Do you want coffee?"

"Yes." She sat up and took my cup, drank, handed it back, and leaned against me, her forehead on my shoulder.

After a minute she said, "It's real, isn't it? It really happened."

"Uh huh."

"I thought for a second when I woke up that it was one of those weird dreams that you think are real, like when you're sick and have a fever. But then I remembered. This is real, isn't it?"

I nodded, and said yeah, and she sighed deeply.

"Everything," she said. "*Everything!*"

Her anguish bit me hard. I stroked her back.

She put her arms around me and held tight. "You're going to do something, aren't you?"

"Uh huh."

"You won't just let the police do it?"

"Denny Linden?" I laughed. "No."

"How do you know a police detective?"

"He went to school with my brother Paul. He's not dumb—maybe he's even a good cop—but he wants it to be me and he won't look for anyone else."

"What will you do?"

"Are you sure you want the answer to this question?"

She leaned back and looked up at me. "Yes."

"I'm going to find my cousin Andonios, Andy to you, in case I need someone to watch my back, and I'm going to find Salter's brother and have a conversation. Ever meet him?"

"Barry's brother? No."

I offered the cup and she drank more coffee. I finished it and set the cup aside.

"After that," I said, "I don't know. I hope it involves a personal encounter. And you," I said, "you must absolutely promise me that you will not leave this apartment today. Not a step, not an inch."

"The show." She pushed me away and tried to get past me and off the bed. "Everything's there—at the gallery—I have to go there. We have to plan where to hang everything."

I stopped her with an arm around her middle. "No, absolutely not. You can call what's-her-name, tell her what happened, tell her you can't come today. It's Sunday. You need a day off."

"Are you sure?"

"Yes, I'm sure. Listen, just do as I say, just this once. Promise me you won't go out today."

"I *always* do as you say. All right, I promise." She flopped back down on the pillow.

"I'll take you there tomorrow."

"All right."

"By the way, you will *not* go to his funeral."

"Right. Yes. I won't."

"You can stay in bed, you know, if you want to. Those black circles are bigger than they were before I took you on the nature walk."

"If I hadn't gone out…"

"Damn it, I knew you were going to say that." I leaned over her, a hand on each side of her head. "If we hadn't gone out, you might be there now, just another little bit of debris."

"You don't know that."

"You don't know any different. Don't be stupid. Stay in bed. Catherine isn't working today and she'll be happy to take care of you. She's a nurse. She's very good at taking care."

"No, no, no, no." She sat up. "No one needs to take care of me."

"Jesus." I threw up my hands. "All right. There's the bathroom, totally private. Wear my clothes if you need anything. I'll probably be gone when you come out, so you can kiss me goodbye now, here where there's no one to see you." I pulled her close, squeezed until she said oof. "I know everything's horrible, but it's a delight to see you in my bed."

2

The office was open for a few hours on Sundays to pay off the players who had winnings coming and couldn't wait until Monday. Two cousins—Peter and Mike—were taking all the incoming calls on cell phones from various locations around the city. Philip came into the office because Paul couldn't be bothered. But it was a bet that Philip would come anyway. Uncle Cy, who was the accounting genius without whom we probably couldn't operate, and who had no other life, he was usually there. Andy or I or both of us would be there riding shotgun—literally. There was a lot of money there on the weekends and no one else in the building. We kept a loaded double-barreled 12-gauge behind the door and three handguns in three different desk drawers. So far we'd never used any of them, but Uncle Cy, who was a Vietnam vet, cleaned and reloaded each of them once a week.

Andy was already in when I got there. So was Philip, and Cy, and so was a box of little cinnamon muffins from Sofia.

Philip said, "How's Clare?"

I said, "Pretty sad, but working her way through it." I took a muffin.

Uncle Cy rarely even listened to us. We had two rooms and he sat at a desk in the first room and kept all the financial information on a computer that updated every five minutes to a website on Mars and would crash immediately and totally if he pushed any of several buttons in the office. At the same time the safe behind him would lock down tight and the door to the corridor would lock also. Another button closed the door to the inner office. He had other lock-ups and lock-downs that he didn't tell even us about. A cop with a warrant or a bad guy with a gun might come in but he, or she, wouldn't get much. Or get out.

Besides, we played poker with, and took bets from, and had photos of, a lot of DAs and cops.

I said, "How long do you want us here?"

"We'll close up in about an hour."

I said to Andy, "Go with me to find Barry Salter's brother? I want to ask him who Barry was working for. And with."

"Sure. Is he a *malaka*, too?"

"Don't know. But my guess is probably. Bring your gat."

We both grinned. He opened his jacket and showed it to me, in his shoulder holster. I went into the outer office and got mine from the safe. I didn't keep it in the apartment because of the kids. I had a shoulder holster in a desk drawer and I put it on.

Harry called. He said, "I just heard about it."

"For Christ's sake, how?"

"I happened to play with a cop. Is she all right? She wasn't there, was she?"

"No, we were out on the river walk. And no, she's not all right. She lost everything."

"Cameras? All of it?"

"Yeah."

"Moth-er-fuck," he said slowly.

"Yeah."

"Where is she?"

"At my sister's."

"Good. If there's someone to beat up, I want in."

"I'll let you know."

Somebody pushed the button on the outside of the main door to the building that sounded a buzzer by Uncle Cy's desk. He in turn pushed a button to activate the intercom and closed-circuit TV. He said, "Yes?"

"Roy Corelli."

"Who's that with you?"

"Fred Gretz."

They were both regulars and Uncle Cy recognized them. He buzzed them into the building and a couple of minutes later they appeared on the monitor from the corridor outside the office. Andy picked up the shotgun and went to stand by the wall. Cy pushed the button that unlocked the door.

Corelli said, "Hi, Andy," and Andy said, "Hey, Roy."

Corelli picked up five hundred and Gretz took home three. Hardly worth coming downtown for. But most of the ones who came in on Sundays had some kind of jones on.

As soon as they left, Philip said, "Forget it, Cy. Close it up." And Cy started tapping keys and pushing buttons without any comment. We heard the safe lock down.

Philip said, "I'm sick of lowlifes. I want to talk to someone outside the business."

Uncle Cy stood in the doorway with his coat on. He said goodnight and left. The door locked behind him.

After a bit I said, "You need a break. Go on a cruise with Sofia. She'd like that. And they have casinos. Or go to Las Vegas."

He said, "With all the other lowlifes."

I said, "Surely not everybody."

Andy said, "You could even retire. You and Sofia would be okay financially. Better than okay. So would Catherine. And Uncle Nick. Uncle Cy could play video games and manage our investments at home on his dining-room table. He's definitely not in this for the action. Not any more, if he ever was."

Philip shook his head. "No, not anymore."

"And neither are you," I said.

He gave me an eyebrows-up look.

Andy said, "Sam and I can keep on playing. And so can you if you want some action."

There was one more thing on our minds. Philip said it. "What about Paul?"

I said, maybe a bit more hotly than I needed to, "If you think we should keep this business going as is just so that bloodsucker can siphon off more money—"

Philip put a hand up and I stopped. "He's family," he said.

"Then he can take his share when we liquidate, just like everyone else."

Andy said, "I'm with Sam on this one."

Philip said, "I'll think about it. Talk it over with Sofia. I'll tell you this much: If this attack on your Clare comes back to this business, we'll do whatever's necessary to make sure it doesn't happen again, even if it means closing up."

3

Andy and I started at a bar across the river where I thought we could get a line on Salter and maybe his brother. I knew very little about Barry Salter, actually, just that he was a creep. He'd tried several times to get into a game with me but I'd managed to duck every one. I figured him for a sore loser. But he'd mentioned this bar. Bragged about playing there.

The bar was called Macreevy's and the kind of place my father had described as "dark as the inside of a doughnut hole". I often wondered where he got those turns of phrase. Maybe he knew more about physics than I thought.

Regardless of the laws against indoor smoking, it was smoky indoors at Macreevy's. There were two basketball games on two TVs and a low thrum of conversations, which died out completely when it became apparent that two strangers were on the premises. We edged our way up the bar between a number of men who weren't moving aside for us.

The bartender looked at us but didn't move in our direction. I took a hundred out of my coat pocket where I had it ready and showed it to him. He came closer.

"I'm looking for Finny Salter," I said.

Andy was half turned away, casually watching everyone else.

"He's waking his brother," the bartender said.

"So soon? I'm surprised his brother's even out of the morgue."

"No comedy," Andy muttered.

The bartender reached for the bill, but I moved it back a bit, just enough. He said, "Well, then, I suppose he's home with his mother."

"Where's that?"

He looked vague. "Up behind the Capitol, I guess."

That was all I was going to get here. I slid the money across and he laid his hand over it. We turned back toward the door and pushed back through the crowd. I was slightly behind Andy. We went out the door fast and trotted across the street faster and scrambled into the car.

Andy got the car going fast and he was out into the traffic and passing other cars before he'd gone two blocks. There were very few cars crossing the bridge and we were able to make sure no one was following us. I slid my gun back into its holster and got out my phone.

Clare finally answered, sounding mostly asleep. "It's me," I said.

"Mm-hmm."

"Listen. Did Salter ever say where his family lived?"

"Um, I think he just had a mother. And his brother."

"Where does his mother live?"

"On Rice Street."

"Do you know the address?"

"No."

Of course she didn't.

"But he drove me by there once. We didn't go in. There was an Italian restaurant and a flower shop and a sort of strip mall. And they lived in an old two-story house painted red."

"I know the place. You're great. I'll see you later."

I put the phone away. "Bless that memory for pictures. Guess where we're going?"

"Where?"

"Rice Street."

"Nooooo," he said. "No. I am not going to Rice Street."

But we did. We drove through downtown, up the hill, skirted the Capitol Building, and there we were, the place the Zandroses had broken out of fourteen years before.

There were a lot of buildings gone and even a few replaced.

"Not looking so bad," I said judiciously, knowing it would annoy him.

"Like painting up an old whore! Jesus, I hate this place."

"It's your heritage."

He said, "Up your heritage."

"And mine. You're right. I hate it too."

We found the house and drove by it twice. There were lights inside but it didn't look like a party was going on.

"Okay," I said, "keep the motor running and your gat out and wait for me."

"You're going in there alone?"

"If I'm not out in five minutes, fire your gun into a snowbank, call 911, and tell 'em you heard shots fired. And when the cops get here, leave."

"Leave you here? And who explains it to Clare? And Philip?"

"Just get the cops here." I got out of the car, leaving the door hanging open, walked up the badly shoveled walk and steps and onto the porch. I didn't see a bell push, so I knocked. After a while a man opened the door. He was large and had big heavy muscles. He looked sort of vaguely like Barry.

"I'm looking for Finny Salter," I said.

"Who're you?"

"Sam Zandros."

He swung at me, meaning to hit me in the belly. He had muscles but he was slow. I sidestepped and he touched me but only barely. However I slipped on some ice. I grabbed his wrist and took him with me as I went backward and over. I kneed him hard in the balls as we went down and managed to throw him off to the side. He got one in on the side of my mouth and I punched him in the nose and felt it go sideways, and then punched the side of his jaw. He got another jab in, to the side of my face, and one into my gut and I rolled free just as Andy put a shot into the snow in the front yard. It sounded like a fucking cannon in the dark late day. Finny rolled the other way and kept going, on his feet but bent over his crotch, and into the house, and I made it back to the car, breathing hard, but intact. I slammed the door and Andy sped away down Rice Street.

"Thanks," I said.

"What the hell happened?" he asked.

"I said my name." I was starting to shake and I hoped I wouldn't throw up. I said, "I think Finny Salter will not be a productive source of information. Are you coming to dinner?"

"No, I have a date with a trio to make a quartet for the evening."

4

I walked into the apartment to find Clare surrounded by my Greek relatives. Philip was there, and Sofia, and their son Jamie and Paul's son Nicky, both four years old and both on Philip's lap. Uncle Nick was there, and two of Catherine's three, Stephen, who was sixteen, and Thomas, who was seven. Sofia and Clare were on the short sofa, and Thomas, beaming, had gotten in between them. He was small, even for our family, and between the voluptuous Sofia and the curvy Clare, he looked like a thatched twig.

I'd caught a look at myself in the hall mirror. My left eye was swollen and purpling up, my upper lip was swollen, and my jaw was scraped and bruised. And my right hand was raw and bloody over my knuckles. My belly hurt. I could only hope that Finny was worse off.

While Clare stared at me, I greeted all my relatives with the usual hugs and kisses. Then I took Clare's right hand in my intact left one and leaned over to speak in her ear. She was wearing a long black skirt and a white satin shirt, which I knew belonged to Catherine, and she was looking very pink.

I said, "See, darling, your champion has returned."

"Are you all right?"

"Not exactly, but nothing permanent. Are you all right?"

"Yes, I am."

"Good."

Catherine came in to announce dinner, and after pulling Clare to her feet, I left her standing where she was, went to the bar cabinet and poured myself a large Balvenie, and came back to lead her to the table. Ioulia, Catherine's daughter, and Meli, Philip's daughter, who were both twelve, appeared from Catherine's room, where they'd apparently been trying various looks with makeup, and the four older kids stood in the corner arguing furiously in sharp whispers over who would sit by Miss Russell.

Catherine said that Miss Russell would sit between me and Sofia. Then she put all six kids across the table from us, where they stood grinning at us, which I was sure Clare found unnerving. I did.

Uncle Nick was at the head of the table and Philip at the other end. Catherine was on the other side of Sofia.

Sofia was plump and dark and beautiful, and the sweetest woman alive. Philip wordlessly adored her. Uncle Nick was taller than me or either of my brothers or Andy, and held himself very erect. He was sixty, but he was still as dark-haired as any of the rest of us. In the presence of the stranger he was formal, polite, and serious. He had the honor of saying grace and blessing the food, which he did in Greek, and we all sat.

Food was passed, and wine, and everyone talked at once.

I got some whisky past the cuts in my mouth, and didn't eat much.

I looked around the table and saw, for the first time, maybe what Clare saw. Dark hair, dark eyes, flashing white teeth, rich warm Mediterranean skin colors. I looked like Philip and Philip looked like Uncle Nick and Catherine looked like me, and Sofia, even though she had married in, carried on the pattern, and all six children were mirrors of the adults.

And Clare might have dark hair but she also had that fair fair porcelain skin and those blue blue eyes. Her hair was fine and soft and curly, and ours was thick and straight or crisply wavy. The men tended to keep it short or it stuck out like the quills on a porcupine. Mine was thick and straight and I brushed it forward, as did Philip and Andy. Sort of an all-purpose short Caesar look. Uncle Nick and Uncle Cy wore very short buzz cuts. I didn't know what mysterious things the women did to tame theirs. Catherine's was very wavy and she wore it in a bun to work but mostly loose and clipped back at home. She was starting to gray, which she complained about, but I rather liked it. Sofia's was some sort of braid in the back and waves and tendrils around her face.

Sofia said to Clare, "You're not used to such a crowd, I know. Sam says you live all alone here. I mean, you have no family in this area."

"Yes, my mother lives in California, but she—we aren't close. And my father died when I was quite young."

Sofia explained some of the recipes and told Clare the Greek names. "Spanakopita. Spinach pie."

Clare said, "Oh, I had that once. But it was in little triangular crusts."

Catherine said, "That's the most popular traditional way to serve it, but I make it like a lasagna and freeze it."

Sofia said, "I'm home more, so I make the little pockets more often."

Clare said, "This is delicious. Much better than the one in the restaurant."

I held a platter for Clare to help herself to a stuffed green pepper.

Sofia said, "Yemista. Sometimes it's a stuffed tomato. We still use the Greek names," she said, almost apologetically. "It's how we grew up."

Clare said, "It's all so good!"

Thomas said loudly to Clare, "Ioulia and Meli have Greek names. But the boys don't. But that's okay because guys at school would be assholes about it."

There was a nanosecond of dead air.

"My name means 'twin'," Thomas said. "I looked it up on the net."

I said, "Two of you? God save us."

Thomas was on a roll. He looked at Clare again. "Is your name really Frances?"

"Yes, I just don't use it. Socially. I use Frances professionally."

He opened his mouth and I said, "Thomas, leave it."

Thomas said quickly, "May we call you Aunt Clare?"

"Yes, if that's what you—"

I was glaring at Thomas. I said, "Catherine, can you speak to him about his manners?"

Sofia handed me a platter. "I approve of Thomas's interest in names."

I said, "It's not his interest, it's his manners."

"I said 'may'," Thomas protested.

"Aunt Clare," said Ioulia, leaning forward and adopting the confidential tone of a TV interviewer, "are you and Theo going to get married?"

Clare said, "Who?"

Thomas said, "Theo."

I said, "Me."

She switched to me. "Theo?"

Catherine said in her firmest voice, "When Stephen was learning to talk, Sam didn't want to be called 'Uncle Sam', for obvious reasons, so we just taught Stephen to say 'Theo', which is Greek for 'uncle'. And the younger ones all followed along. And that will be all on that subject."

Thomas said, "Are you already married? Because I saw you were sleeping in Theo's bed."

Clare began laughing into her napkin, then laughing and crying both at once. She turned toward me and tried to leave her chair, but I caught her arms and held her until Catherine and Sofia were there to go with her. Philip got up after them and closed the glass doors between the living room and dining room, and I stood up and drained my whisky glass, which stung like hell.

I leaned forward on my good hand and fixed my eye on Thomas.

"That woman," I said as distinctly as I could past my cut mouth, "who I care about more than anyone or anything in this world, lost everything she had, everything, all of it, and she had got every bit of it on her own." All six sets of eyes were wide. "She was *given* nothing! You—" I waved my arm to include them all. "You have been *given everything*, and you see fit to—to *insult* her—with your rude questions and lack of respect for a woman who is my guest in this house—" I threw up my empty hand. "Fuck." I sat down, filled my glass with wine, and closed my eyes.

Ioulia cleared her throat and said, "I'm sorry."

"I am, too," Meli said, somewhat unnecessarily.

Thomas said, "I'm sorry, too. It's just so exciting to *see* Aunt Clare and—"

Philip said, "Thomas, go finish eating in the kitchen. All of you go."

They filed out, to the kitchen, taking their plates with them, and shut the door behind themselves.

"Nice speech," Philip said dryly.

"Did it work?"

"Worked on me. What happened? Today."

I stood up, walked around a bit. "We found Finny Salter. Don't ever go to a bar called Macreevy's." I told them about the bartender and my call to Clare. "So we found him. On fucking Rice Street. He didn't want to talk to me." I described my encounter with Finny.

"Is he alive?"

"Oh yeah. Perhaps he'll never be a father. That would be best."

Philip passed around his tin of small cigars and we all three lit up.

Philip said, "Why is she a target?"

I said, "That's the question, isn't it? I wish I knew. Except for a few ill-advised dates with Barry Salter, I don't see any way that Clare is connected to that social scene."

Then Philip asked, "Do you think the Salters, at least the one who's dead, might have been working for someone?"

"I've got no idea. Why? Does that make sense?"

"It might." He shoved his plate aside, went to the sideboard, put out his cigar, and began cutting a chocolate cake into slices. He served the three of us. "Paul and I got a visit, at the office, this morning. From a representative of Kevvy Smith." Philip smiled. "That's what he called himself, a representative. A group from Chicago is trying to move into St. Paul. Kevvy wants our neutrality."

"We've always been neutral. We're not an organization, we're just a family. A family business. Kevvy Smith knows we don't count." I put aside tobacco for chocolate, swallowed some wine to cleanse my palate, and picked up my dessert plate.

He said, "Maybe these new people don't know that."

"And Clare's easy to get at."

Philip nodded. "Yes. Very."

I said, "But no message, no warning?"

"Have you been back there?"

"No."

He said, "Well, go. Tomorrow. Look at her mail."

I stopped prowling. "She's a very private person."

"And still alive. Look at her damned mail."

"All right. What does Paul say?"

"Not much. Wait and see. But he's acting like he's lying about something. Hiding something. You know how he is."

I did. Paul was the world's worst liar. "Hiding what?"

Philip shook his head. "No idea."

Uncle Nick gestured with his cigar. "If Salter *was* working for someone, we have to decide how to answer his boss. Find out from Kevvy who it is. We'll think about what to do next. We need to know if it's dangerous for your young woman. Is she going to marry you?"

I went to the sideboard and splashed ouzo into my empty whisky glass and added water. "Why don't we just get her in here and you can ask her. You can ask her about her family, her dowry, can she have children, all that stuff. We can look at her teeth."

Uncle Nick reached up, put his hand on my shoulder and squeezed.

I started to pace again. "She's very stubborn."

Uncle Nick shook his head. "And very courageous. Especially such a young woman."

I grinned. "You were born in the wrong century, Uncle Nick."

"I read the newspapers and watch TV and I know what I know."

Catherine came in through the glass doors. "She's all right," she said before I could ask. "She's had her hysterics…"

"About time."

"…and she's done crying. She wants to see you."

5

Clare was sitting in the middle of my bed, my comforter around her, her eyes red and puffy. I sat next to her, leaned against the headboard, pulled her down against my chest, and rubbed her back.

"I'm sorry to be such a baby in front of your family," she said.

"If you hadn't let loose, they'd have decided you didn't care. Or you were crazy. Or a bit lacking."

"Maybe I am. Maybe it's all stupid, taking pictures. Maybe I'm better off without all that stuff."

"Yeah, right."

She rubbed her face on my shirt. "Where did you get the ones on your wall here, the ones I took?"

"The one of me you gave me. The others I liberated from your workroom. You were discarding them. I have some others, put away. You're learning all my secrets."

"And what about the ones of me that Gerald Martin took?"

"I commissioned them. It was my first venture as patron of the arts."

She sighed. She said, "Today, after you left, I went out to the kitchen and Catherine gave me something to eat—she made the most wonderful sticky buns and I was so hungry—I ate two—and she fixed me eggs and she told me that she's a nurse and that I needed to spend the day resting, maybe two days, to heal—repair—from the shock —so I came back in here and before I went to sleep I looked at your room. And I took pictures of it, just with my phone, but that always helps me look at things. I like how large it is and what a high ceiling it has and the tall windows. And I like your rugs—the colors, the patterns—blue and cream and dark red. And your walls like warm cream and your mission-style furniture and your paintings—is that a Donnie Brooks?"

I said yes. I was becoming hypnotized by her dreamy voice.

"I knew you would have books—many books—and you do. And I looked at your desk. And I thought about how I know every bit of you—I mean your body—all your muscles and bones—but I was sort of embarrassed to be curious about what was on the top of your desk. But I looked anyway. Shall I tell you?"

How much wine had she had? At least one before dinner, one with dinner, not much food.

I said yes again.

Her eyes were closed. "I saw pens and pencils and several notepads. And I saw a book on logic and a book on probability. And four decks of cards and a little digital recorder, and a glass piggy bank full of pennies. And a miniature painting of the Blessed Virgin on an easel."

She sighed again. I was afraid to move, to breathe.

She said, "It was so *intense*, trying to make my own studio, and everything else got pushed aside. But you were there." She turned her face into my shoulder. "I've been—I don't know how to say this."

"You're doing fine so far."

"I've been careless. Of you. Hurting you. I'm sorry."

"Clare—"

She tilted her face up and kissed me on the chin and put her fingers over my mouth. "Don't say anything—let me talk, just this once." I rolled my eyes. "When I see your family, it's almost like I can *see* the love. Almost like I could photograph it. Then I realized that I want to tell you—I figured it out a long time ago, but I didn't know what to say. And it seems—the word doesn't seem like enough, somehow, to describe what I feel about you—when I think about you or see you—"

I pulled her hand away. "Clare, in about ten seconds I'm going to become dangerous."

"It's I love you. Wait, I'm not done."

But my mouth was on hers and she gave up. I stood up and pulled her to her feet and we undressed each other, touching, rubbing, caressing, until I took her back onto the bed. I felt the exhaustion in both of us give way to pleasure. When we were done she shivered and I pulled the comforter around her and leaned on one elbow next to her, kissed her nose, twisted my fingers in her hair.

"You are the only woman in my bed here ever," I said.

6

I held her while she wept a bit more for her cameras. Then she stopped crying and eventually her arms loosened and she fell asleep. I held her until her breathing was slow and easy and deep and all her muscles were limp, and then let her down onto the pillow and carefully pulled my arm from under her. She stirred and murmured and I kept my hands on her until she was quiet again. Then I put on pants and shirt and went barefoot into the living room. Catherine, Stephen, and Ioulia were there, snugged up on the long couch together, watching television.

I flopped down on the short sofa.

Catherine said, "Uncle Nick says you're to call him tomorrow to tell him how Clare's doing."

I raised an eyebrow. "Uncle Nick wants to know how she is."

"Yes."

Ioulia said, "How can Miss Russell not have a family? Mom says she doesn't have a family, but she must have."

"Maybe, maybe not. Lots of people have small families and if they die or lose track—" I shrugged. "Her mother is probably still alive, but Clare doesn't know for sure."

Ioulia wrinkled her forehead and looked horrified.

I said roughly, "She never wanted Clare and she neglected her and was glad to get rid of her when she was sixteen."

Catherine put her arm around Ioulia and squeezed her.

"Is she all right?" Catherine asked me.

"She's asleep."

"Do you want some ointment for your face?"

"I have some. She's going to need clothes. Will you take her shopping? I'll give you the money. Do you work tomorrow?"

"No, I'm not on duty until Tuesday. Yes, I can do that, if she'll let me."

"I'll talk her into it."

"I have things she can wear. We're the same height, although she's thinner. She ate almost nothing."

"Usually she eats like a little horse." I laughed. "She was feeling surrounded."

The TV show ended. Catherine said, "Stephen, Ioulia, your bedtime."

Unselfconsciously, Stephen and Ioulia kissed both me and Catherine goodnight.

"Is there coffee?" I asked Catherine when we were alone. She nodded and we both went into the kitchen.

She poured coffee. "She does love you, Sam. It's so clear when she looks at you."

"Of course she does," I said lightly.

But I think she saw the tears in my eyes as I turned away. She said, "She's like a little moth and you're her light."

"Oh God, Catherine." I gulped coffee. "You sounded just like Mama."

She said, "I wish she were here to see Clare, to meet her. She'd be so happy."

I said, "She would, wouldn't she? She really would."

7

In my room Clare was very sound asleep. I had a missed-call number on my phone and I plugged in a cable and pushed a button to turn on a RECORD function in my cell phone, and punched in the number.

"Yeah?"

"This is Sam Zandros."

"Wait a minute."

Then a new voice, whisky-rough, deliberate, authoritative. "Zandros."

"Who's this?"

"Kevvy Smith."

"Hello, Kevvy."

He said, "I hear a friend of yours had some trouble."

Anger and frustration turned my stomach over. I could hear Clare breathing. "I'm taking care of it, Kevvy."

"Well, I know you would, Sam, but I think maybe you can't."

"Why not?"

"This Salter is working for a man in Chicago who's a competitor of mine who wants to pick up some business in St. Paul."

"*Was* working. Who was he working for?"

"The people from Chicago, they haven't been in touch with you?"

"No."

"They will be. I'd hate to see you on the wrong side."

"Kevvy, I'm not on any side. I never have been. You know that. Nobody in my family has. Your business is not ours. But you're not telling me anything, Kevvy. Who was with him and who was he working for?"

"I think your best bet, Sam, will be to keep your family out of everyone's way until I can deal with this competitor."

"I believe you, Kevvy, but believe me, too. We are not part of this."

"Just stay clear."

"Let me know?"

"Sure." He hung up.

I took a shower to wash away the phone call, dabbed ointment on my cuts and scrapes, and crawled in beside Clare.

Monday, February 27

1

I woke up at seven and heard the shower running. I dozed again and woke up and this time she was gone from the room. I pulled on a pair of levis and a sweater and went looking for her. She was in the kitchen, wearing my fleece robe, drinking coffee and juice with Catherine. She looked up when I came in and the look on her face when she saw me, and her smile, made something catch in my chest. Catherine was dishing up scrambled eggs for her onto a plate that held a buttered corn muffin.

I turned a chair around next to her, straddled it, and leaned over the back of it to kiss her cheek. "You look rested," I said.

Catherine put a glass of juice in front of me.

"I feel like a real person today," Clare said. "Yesterday I felt like some sort of robot." She drank coffee. "You promised you would take me to the gallery today."

"But not at eight in the morning. What time do you think Ms. Bragg gets there?"

"She's closed on Mondays, but she said she'd be there at about two."

"I have time for breakfast then," I said. "Will you let me buy you some clothes today?"

"Is this another favor, like the money one?"

"Yes, very like it." She opened her mouth and I held up a hand. "No speeches. I'm not in the mood. Just say yes, and you and Catherine can take all or most of my money and go somewhere and spend it. I have other things to do this morning and I'll meet you at the gallery later. Like about three. There can't be that much for you to do there. Then back here for dinner and then we can maybe go to a movie."

"Good Lord, you have my whole day planned."

I leaned over to speak in her ear. "And night."

"But I don't need to take up Catherine's day. I can shop by myself. For that matter, I can go to the gallery by myself if you have other things to do."

"Listen, Frances Clare. I know you. If you go shopping by yourself, you'll buy a pair of socks and quit."

She told me once that she didn't know how to shop. No one ever showed her. I figured a day with Catherine would be a good first lesson.

I said, "You need something sexy and arty for your opening and then you need the sweet little things to wear under it. Am I right?"

"Oh, aren't you always? All right."

"Have you called your insurance company?"

She shook her head.

"Do you know who to call?"

"I don't remember his name. It's at home. In my desk. I don't want to go there."

"I'll get it. I'll go by there today and find it."

She stood up. "There's a folder that says 'Insurance'. Or there was. I'm going to get dressed."

I watched her go, listening until I heard the door to my room close behind her.

"This vandalism," I said to Catherine, "maybe it wasn't just private vengeance aimed at Clare. Maybe it's someone trying to get at us—maybe me—through her."

Catherine looked shocked. "Who?"

"I don't know yet. I'll tell you all about it later. But Clare can't know about it. She wouldn't know how to handle it."

She frowned. "I think she could. You should tell her. She has a right to know. It was her place."

"Well, I don't think she could, and I'm not going to tell her. I'm going to call Andonios. If you see him today, don't do anything elusive. Where shall I have him find you?"

She thought a moment. "We'll start at Jo Webster's. Ten o'clock, or a little after. But Sam, what about the children? What about Sofia, and Lillian?"

"I don't know. I don't know anything yet. Clare was easy to find, easy to get at, and they had a willing creep. I don't even know what they want. I got the news sort of roundabout. All I know—I think—is that she's a target right now on our behalf. Maybe."

"I'll be careful. But you've got to do something about the children."

"I will, I will. I'm going to see Philip as soon as I dress. Now. I'm going now."

2

At three o'clock I was standing in front of the gallery, waiting for Clare, running everything through my mind again. Andonios had been sent for and presumably had been hovering around Catherine and Clare all day. I'd gone to see Philip and Paul and Uncle Nick at the office, and they had listened to the tape of my phone conversation with Kevvy Smith. Cousins Pete and Mike were keeping watch outside the school that all the children attended and picking them up at school doors. The guard service we used in all the apartment buildings had been alerted and the staffing beefed up.

I'd been to her house. In the cold daylight the wreckage was even more appalling and it was starting to smell bad, even though the heat had been off since we left there on Saturday. I found the insurance folder, wandered through the rooms, picked up a few prints in her workroom that had escaped, found a silver bracelet unharmed on her bedroom floor. I went down to the deli for coffee and sat at the counter where it was warm and smelled good, and called her insurance rep and agreed to meet the claims adjustor the next day at her house. I convinced him

Clare didn't need to be there but promised that she would call to authorize me to start the claims process. I arranged for guards to be on duty at the gallery and for Ellie Bragg to tell Clare that it was Ellie's idea. Ellie thought it was very exciting.

I emptied Clare's mailbox, which still held Saturday's and now Monday's deliveries, and went through those and all the recent-looking papers in and on and around her desk, but I didn't find anything to explain what was happening. I took her mail with me when I left.

Just before coming to the gallery, I went to a lingerie shop I knew about and bought a black silk chemise that I thought would fit her. The young woman who waited on me had all but offered to model it.

They arrived in a taxi, Catherine and Clare in back, Andonios in front next to the driver. I grinned at him as I opened both doors.

"She spotted you, didn't she?" I jeered as Andy and Clare got out, then stuck my head into the back seat. "Everything okay?" I asked Catherine.

"She's happy, I'm exhausted, Andy is embarrassed, and you are broke." She laughed. "I'm going home to make dinner. Andy's invited, so bring him with you."

I handed her the lingerie box and gave the driver fifty bucks and stepped back to shut the door. Clare and Andy had already gone into the gallery and I followed them. When I closed the door behind me, she was across the large room. She turned and looked at me with the same smile I had seen that morning. My awareness of her filled me and I wondered how any one woman could thrill me so.

She was wearing a new silky black down-filled below-the-knees belted coat with a fur-trimmed hood, and shiny black boots and black trousers. A long black scarf hung around her neck.

"You look like a licorice stick," I said.

"No sane woman could resist your compliments," she said. "A man kept following us and I said to Catherine, there's a man following us, he looks like Sam, and she said, yes, that's Andy, and invited him to lunch. Imagine my surprise. We made him carry everything, and Andy and I are going to Belize."

Andy and I grinned at each other.

"I'm going to find Ellie," she said, and went up the stairs at the back of the room.

We lounged near the doorway. "Well," Andy said, "I'm still a bit new at this surveillance stuff, but I'll catch on." He waved his arm at the gallery full of huge colorful—but not the natural colors—photographs of flowers. "I suppose this is art?"

"I suppose so. You'll have to ask Clare. My study of post-Renaissance art ended the day I graduated. I hope you didn't scare her too much."

"If I did, she didn't mention it. What the hell is going on?"

"I don't know. Someone's trying to move in on Kevvy Smith and somehow we got in the middle and I got her in the middle."

"This is not exactly our game. Wars, I mean." Andy eyed a spiky welded-metal sculpture on a pedestal by the door. "Why aren't you telling her what's going on? It'd be easier. And safer."

"I don't think she could handle it. She doesn't have any experience with creeps like Kevvy and his ilk."

He said, "Let's go outside for a minute."

We stepped out, walked over to stand by the curb.

Andy said, "She doesn't strike me as stupid."

I gave him an angry look.

"It's you who can't handle it, cousin," he said. "You're afraid she'll turn around to you and say what the hell have you gotten me into. They had that Salter bastard handy, but she's not in the front of the line because of him. She's there because you put her there." He backed up a step. "I'll fight you if I have to, you know I will, but I'd rather not. It hurts my hands."

I looked at my own fists, took a deep breath, let it out, and straightened my fingers. "Sorry," I said. "You just don't know her. She's—she thinks you can pretend things away. There are a lot of things she doesn't want to know about, some of them about me, so she just doesn't. They don't exist."

"I know more about her than you think I do," said Andy, rather surprisingly. "We have some mutual acquaintances besides you. I know what you're talking about. She lives on the edge of being outside and she has a great smile and she doesn't let anybody in. I know someone who thinks she's ice all the way through."

"Because she's so easy to hurt."

"You've been taking care of her, but this time you're just putting her further out in front if you don't let her know what's going on. And you may be making it worse for the rest of us. Besides, she deserves to know. She has a right to know."

I watched cars drive by. He'd said pretty much what Catherine had said. "What do the others think?" I asked.

"I don't know, but eight to one they agree with me."

"Yeah. All right. But not until after her opening. I can't mess that up. I can't distract her now. Here she comes."

<h1 style="text-align:center">3</h1>

At Catherine's I took the new coat and admired the new gray and white striped shirt she was wearing with the new black trousers. I brought beers from the kitchen and sat next to her on the couch and listened to Thomas describe a school assignment for which he was planning to write a report on the Trojan War and, with some astonishment, listened to Andonios recite, in classical Greek, a part of the Iliad—Nestor urging Patroclus to beg Achilles to fight. Thomas and Clare were entranced. So was Kori, the lovely and deceptively demure dark-haired beauty Andy'd been leading down the garden path almost since high school. Her high school. If he could get it together to love her as much as he loved his saxophone and his music, they'd have been married by then and she'd have been round as a pumpkin. Even though her mother was against the union—something about gambling. But he didn't want to push Kori.

Philip and Sofia arrived, with Jamie and Meli, and Uncle Nick, who kissed Clare's cheek. To my surprise, she kissed him back. Stephen and Ioulia finished their homework and came in. Catherine came for a quick glass of white wine at the last minute. With each new arrival, Clare moved closer to me. I had my arm firmly around her shoulders.

To my relief, all the children were sent to eat in the kitchen. Clare sat between me and Sofia again. After a while the noise and confusion of several conversations going at once began to overwhelm her, and I felt her shrinking toward me. I put my hand in the middle of her back, poured wine in her glass, and muttered next to her ear, "You look absolutely smashing and I can see down your shirt," and laughed when she went pink and sat up straight. Andy smiled and raised his glass from across the table.

4

As we were leaving the table, she whispered to me, "I need to do something *normal!*" So we went to Vincent's. We sat at the bar and she leaned against me and I looked down at her and laughed. "Your shirt is open, you wanton." I reached around and buttoned her up.

Mead the bartender leaned on his elbows across the bar from us. He said, "Aren't you two old enough to wait until you get home?" She started laughing again and Mead grinned. "I can't serve her. She's drunk."

"She had only two glasses of wine," I said. "I poured them myself."

"What happened to your face? That's a very fine mouse."

Clare said, "He got stuck in a revolving door," and fell against me, helpless with laughter. I had to put out an arm to keep her from falling off the barstool.

I said, "Two small Summits," to Mead. He shook his head at her and set two small glasses of beer in front of us. "I heard what happened. I hope someone else's face is in worse shape than yours."

I said, "Maybe not his face, but definitely his balls."

"Anyone we know?"

"Barry Salter's brother, Finny. You know him?"

"Don't think so." He patted Clare's hand and went down the bar.

I put my hand on the back of her neck. "Always embarrassing me."

People we knew started coming into the bar and as the evening went on I wondered if everyone we knew was going to stop in at Vincent's to stand awkwardly by the bar and tell her what a horrible thing it was. No one talked long—no one really knew what to say about an event so contrary to what their world was supposed to be like.

At last she asked, "Can we leave?" and I stood up, put some money on the bar, and helped her into her coat, and we went.

5

Later, in my room, I said, "That's pretty hard for you, all those people."

"It was all right with you there."

TUESDAY, FEBRUARY 28

1

In the morning she was someplace else, out of reach.

Catherine and the children were gone when I went to the kitchen for coffee, and I brought two cups back to my room. She was in the shower, and came out in my robe, a towel on her head, and stood staring out the window. I drank coffee and looked at her back.

"What's the matter?" I asked.

"I want to go home."

"Darling, you can't."

"But I want to." She turned around and looked at me angrily.

I said, "Maybe if you stamp your foot."

"Did you get my insurance papers?"

"Uh huh. I'm meeting the claims agent at ten."

"You are? What about me? Who the hell do you think you are? This is my business. Those are my cameras and my pictures and my clothes and... and mine. God *damn* it. It's all mine. Leave me alone." She picked up the other coffee cup and began to drink. "I'm coming with you."

"I won't leave you alone but you can come along. Of course you can. I thought it would be too hard for you."

"You could ask."

"Okay, I could ask. Get dressed then."

"I can't. I haven't anything to wear."

I gestured at the pile of boxes on my desk. "What's in there?"

"Not everyday kinds of stuff."

"Do you have some jeans or something? Those black ones you were wearing yesterday?"

"Yes. All right. But not the shirt."

"Okay, I'll find you a shirt. Do you need socks?"

"Yes."

"Shorts?"

"Very funny." She sat down on the edge of the bed.

"But first—" I found the lingerie-store box. "Open this."

She did and drew out the black chemise and held it up. "Oooh."

"Put it on." I pulled the towel off her head and reached out to untie the robe's belt, pushed it off her shoulders.

She slid the chemise over her head and arms and I helped her pull it down over her breasts. It was just slightly snug over them and her nipples were bumps in the silk. I ran my fingertips over them and she shivered and licked her lips. She pushed her hands under my T-shirt and ran her palms over my chest.

"You have the most wonderful body," she said. "When I first saw you, I used to, um, daydream about you."

"When was that?"

"You came into the Rattle Rat a few times before Harry introduced us. With him. And once with some woman."

"You didn't think maybe I was a bit skinny?"

"Stop fishing. You were excellent. And you had that way of walking, sort of springy. You still do. And a few times in Vincent's. Didn't you see me?"

"I think I was only seeing myself then. But I must have met you right after that."

"Harry is such a joker. I think he saw me looking at you."

I tipped her over on the bed, dropped my pajama pants, and came down on top of her. I put my hands under her hips and moved into her and heard, with ever-undiminished pleasure, the noise she always made in the bottom of her throat at that moment.

I went up on my elbows and watched her face and saw my own movements reflected there. Not to put too fine a point on it, I was a skillful lover and I knew it and liked that about myself, and I liked giving women pleasure and sometimes I could manipulate them with it and I knew that, too, and didn't like it as much. But with Clare, there was something else.

I tried never to trespass on any of her fears, never acknowledging or showing any awareness of them. I also knew how profoundly hurt she would be if I ever forced her or manipulated her, and I knew how easily I could do it if I chose to. I thought I knew the line between giving her pleasure and using that pleasure. And sometimes, like now, I watched her face and skirted the line, wanting to use this, to tie her to me, to end the tension brought on by her indecision, by the possibility that she could walk out of my life.

She put her arms up to me and I buried my face in the curve of her neck and shoulder.

2

The claims agent pulled up right behind us in front of her house. He viewed the wreckage calmly and took notes and photos, and asked Clare a number of questions about her cameras and other photographic equipment. He took Denny Linden's name and number, said he would arrange for copies of the police reports and photos, and offered to arrange for a cleaning crew. Clare looked around and accepted and he left.

She was standing in the middle of her workroom. "I think there are a few things here to salvage," she said. "Prints. Negatives. Most of my negatives, actually."

"Well, let's get them out of here today. Tomorrow the heavy equipment comes in and everything goes out."

I brought some cardboard cartons she had been storing in the back hallway and she started digging about. I poked around in the kitchen, retrieved a few unbroken dishes and most of her flatware and cooking equipment, and stacked them in the sink to be washed. Her desk was still in one piece and I stuffed all her intact papers into the drawers and put a DO NOT TOUCH sign on top.

I said, "I'm putting your CPU into the trunk. Uncle Cy may be able to salvage your hard drive."

Her large heavy wood and metal worktable, too large and heavy to have been destroyed, was still in her workroom, still usable. I put a sign on it, too,

Then I wandered into her studio, saw the mail carrier go by, and brought in her mail. There was nothing of interest to me. No warnings written in crayon in big block letters.

She found quite a lot to salvage in the bathroom, a testament to unbreakable plastic bottles, but nothing in the bedroom.

"Why did he have to take my jewelry?" she asked bitterly. "It wasn't worth anything, not to him."

"He probably threw it away," I said. "Here, I found this when I was here yesterday." I handed her the bracelet I'd picked up the day before.

"And I alone survived," she said. It was a plain silver chain of flat links, and she fastened it onto her wrist. "There was a pair of earrings I always wore with it. They were one of my favorite pairs. I'd like to kill him."

"No, you wouldn't. You wouldn't like how you felt afterward."

"How do you know? I might like it just fine."

After a while she went into the studio. I left her alone until I heard her sniffle, then went in to hold her.

"Do you have a handkerchief?" she asked finally.

I said, "I've started carrying two at all times," and while she blew her nose and wiped her face, I rubbed her back.

She searched the room and found a lens.

3

We put all the boxes into the back hallway with DO NOT TOUCH signs, and drove to Vincent's to eat lunch. When our beers came, she leaned forward and looked up at me across the table.

"What would the wedding be like if we got married?" she asked.

I grinned at her. "A Greek wedding? The experience of a lifetime. You'd never get over it."

"Never?"

"Never. Greek food, Greek wine, ouzo, Greek music, dancing—"

"No rock 'n' roll?"

"Yes, just for you. Greek rock 'n' roll."

"What will I wear?"

"You will wear a white lace dress."

"With a slip."

"And a white veil and pearl earrings. I'll be giving you the pearl earrings."

"Won't your family be scandalized if I wear white?"

"This is our wedding and if we say white, it's white."

"You mean, as usual, if you say it."

"Let me know when you disagree. Then, at some suitable hour, I carry you away to the accompaniment of many lewd jokes."

"And whistles and noisemakers?"

"If you like. After that I have about twelve hours in which to get you pregnant or never hold up my head again."

"I take it the wedding day is chosen to coincide with my fertile time."

"All done very scientifically." I took her hands in mine and kissed her fingertips. "Does this mean you'll marry me?"

"I'm—I'm thinking about it. That's what I promised."

"So you did." I went back to my story. "Then Catherine and Sofia would take over and teach you to cook and in two years you would be more Greek than I am."

"I don't mind being Greek, but I don't want to cook."

"Right, why start now? Forget cooking."

"What would my name be?"

"For Christ's sake, your name can be Queen Elizabeth the Third if you want it to be," I said hotly.

"Come on, just tell me."

"At home you can be Clare Alexandros and at your studio you can be Frances Russell. And there might be a few people who think you're Mrs. Zandros. Would that be satisfactory?"

"I'd still have my studio then?"

"If you want it, of course. Who am I, Attila?"

My burger and her grilled cheese-and-tomato arrived.

"Why all the questions?" I asked.

"One needs data."

I said, "Clare, we can live however we want to. Being married isn't the same as being swallowed whole."

"For some people it is."

"Not for you or me."

"Maybe we couldn't help it."

"Trust me. I will not swallow you whole. And you could never keep me down."

"Tell me about Andonios. Where is Belize, anyway?"

"Central America. It's always hot and it rains every day and it's populated entirely by alligators. Or maybe it's crocodiles. You'd hate it. Andy's my cousin. First cousin. His father and mine were brothers. He's also my age, unlike my own brothers, who are ten and twelve years older, so he and I have always been closer than I ever was to Philip or Paul. Of course Paul is a dick and I was never on good terms with him."

She smiled. All her attention was on me and I liked that extremely.

"Andy and I were together all the way through the university. He started living with my family when we were six. His parents died in a car accident."

"The poor child!"

"Yeah."

"Why have I never seen him before?"

"For one thing, because he hangs out with musicians and I don't. He's a jazz saxophonist besides working in the family business."

"What's another thing?"

"You never wanted anything to do with my family."

"You make me sound hostile."

"No, you were never that. But you made it plain that families were not up for discussion, or even casual conversation."

She said, "I didn't know how to take them. Families, I mean. They seemed so... sticky."

"They can be."

"And now I find I didn't know anything about you. I didn't know where you lived, if you even had a home. Maybe I thought you didn't live anywhere." She drank some beer and sighed. "You must think I'm the most selfish, self-centered person in the whole world."

"No, I just think that's how you cope. It's just you."

"Will you ask them, your family, to the opening? I don't know how to ask them, but I would like them to come, if they want to."

"They will."

"Where's Catherine's husband?"

"He's dead." I watched her face for a while. "Do you really want to know about it?"

She hesitated, then said, "Yes."

"All right. He died in prison. Murdered."

Her face went blank.

"He was in prison for tax evasion. It's something of an occupational hazard in our business."

"Business. You keep calling it that."

"That's what it is. The men get up in the morning and go to the office and the office happens to be a betting shop. Some families sell groceries, some have restaurants, we make book."

"Grocery stores and restaurants aren't illegal."

"You said it didn't bother you."

"'Bother' is not the word. 'Scare', maybe." She turned her hand, still in mine, and held on hard. "I don't want you to go to prison."

"I won't. I have some very nice bookkeeping and I pay a lot of taxes. Playing cards for money may be mildly illegal, but the district attorney would get laughed out of town if he tried to prosecute me. His friends all play with me and he does, too."

"Poor Catherine." Her voice was very soft.

"It was hard for her. Very hard. It was about four years ago, so she had three young children. That's one reason I live there, to be there for them." I rubbed my eyes. "She adored him. Stephanios Kamariotis. We called him The Bull. He wasn't real tall, but he was big. Strong. You should have heard them fight. World-class."

"What did they fight about?"

I had a lot of practice keeping a poker face and I used it now. "She wanted him to leave the business. Do something else."

She pushed her plate away. "And what if we were married and had children and you—and that happened to you? I do know one thing about families and that's what it feels like when your father dies when you're five years old."

"I could step in front of a bus tomorrow."

"That's different! That's not getting murdered in prison!"

"That's not going to happen to me."

"So you say, but you don't know!"

"So I'll do something else. I'll quit."

"No, no, no! Not for me."

"I've thought about it," I said slowly.

"But if you did it for *my* sake—don't you see? I don't want that kind of power!"

I threw up my hands and stood up. "Let's go, before I cause a scene in public." I tossed some money on the table and she stood and stalked angrily out the back door. I followed.

In her car I turned to face her. "Do you want to talk about it anymore?"

She was sitting bolt upright, looking straight ahead through the windshield. "No."

I reached over to her, wound a finger in her curls, and stroked her cheek with my thumb.

She tightened her lips and shook my hand away.

I felt the anger wash through me and I took her wrists in my hands and turned her around to face me. Her eyes were wide and startled. I took a deep breath and let go of her.

"That's thirty-five centuries of Greek manhood getting what it wants," I said in a shaky voice. "It's built in."

"I know."

"And if you push me hard enough, you're apt to run into it."

"I saw it before."

"You did?"

She dropped her eyes. "It's part of you. I saw it."

"Is that so?"

"It's—interesting."

I leaned forward, kissed her cheek, her ear. "Is it?"

She sighed. "You're going to take advantage of this, aren't you? You rat."

I was laughing. "No, never, I promise."

4

When I parked her car in the apartment building garage, she made no move to unbuckle her seatbelt.

She said, "You have a reserved parking place with your name on it but you don't have a car. You've never had one."

I said, "What if I get one? I'll need a place to put it."

After a minute she said, "I'm tired. And I don't think I can face a bunch of people. And the gallery closes at seven and then we're going to start hanging the show."

"Well, you can't sit here until seven. Can you face me?"

"I don't know. Maybe not."

"Come upstairs, go to my room, and stay there. Or go in the guest room if you'd rather. Take a nap. You probably need one. I'll bring you a tray later, and when you want to go to the gallery, I'll take you there. I'm going over to the office, but I won't be long."

I walked. If I had a passion for something physical, besides sex, it was for walking. I usually walked miles every day, a lot of them at night, not on any set route or for any set distance, but just for the walking.

I thought while I walked, but I didn't use it to think, just took what came. Today I thought about Clare, and about marrying her, and about being married to her—these things I'd thought about before—and about what being married to me might be like for Clare. This I hadn't thought about before.

Today the office was not the welcoming place that it usually was for me. I stood at a window, looking out but not interested in what I was seeing. My attention was on Philip and Paul, behind me. I had hoped to find only Philip at the office, and definitely not Paul, but my luck wasn't in. I turned around.

Paul said, "You're joking."

"No. I'm not. I'm thinking of quitting."

"So the old man was right about you."

I said, "What old man?"

Philip put a warning hand on Paul's arm, but he kept talking.

"Who do you think, genius? He said you were soft, we should look out for you." He made a spitting motion.

Philip said, "Paul, shut up."

I looked at Philip.

"No, that's not what he said," Philip said.

"What did he say?"

"He said—you didn't always know the difference between honor and pride."

Paul made a rude noise.

I said dryly, "Yeah, I'll bet he did."

"You were still a kid," Philip said. "In high school."

Paul mimicked spitting again. "A brat. And you still are. So get out then. All you ever think about is yourself. You and fucking Andy. Me and Philip, we got families—and what about Catherine—and Uncle Nick—but do you care? No, it's just you and that bitch with the cameras—"

I was on him before he could blink. I slapped him hard, first with one hand, then the other, and he staggered backward. His reaction was slow, clumsy. He lunged, tried to hit me but missed. I slapped him again. Then Philip pulled him away, and I let him.

Paul rubbed his face but stayed back. "Fuckin' little bastard!"

I laughed. Philip pushed me into the outer room of the office and shut the door behind us. He started to speak, then just threw up his hands.

Finally he found his voice. "Listen, don't pay any attention to him. You want to quit, you quit. We don't need the money."

Uncle Cy must have been in the men's room.

I said, "He's a complete shit, but he might be right."

"No, he's not right. I look at the damn books every day."

"You're sure?"

"Of course I'm sure. It's—"

"What?"

"Two things. I don't want you to quit. I like that it's family. I always have. And what the hell would you do?"

5

"She's feeling surrounded," I told Catherine. "She needs some privacy." I took a carrot from the cutting board.

"And she doesn't need Thomas's latest enthusiasm. He was so impressed by Andy last night that he's decided to read the Iliad in Greek."

"Does he know enough Greek?"

"Certainly not classical Greek. But you know him."

Stephen ushered Andy into the kitchen, then hovered until Catherine told him to go set the table. He didn't answer her but turned to me. He said, "Something's happening, and I want to know what it is. I'm old enough. I want to help."

I said, "You're not old enough, and if your mother wants you to know, she'll tell you."

"But you're the man of the house."

I gave him a sympathetic grin. "Don't pull that shit on me. You know who the head of this household is."

"Out," said Catherine, and Stephen left in a teen-age huff.

"I think you should tell him," said Andy.

I said, "You think everybody should tell everyone everything,"

"Philip and Uncle Nick think that Clare should be told what's going on. It's too dangerous your way. Kevvy could set something up and she could walk right into it."

Catherine was nodding her agreement.

I said, "Thursday. I'll tell her Thursday morning. But not before."

Andy shrugged. "We won't say anything before then, but you're wrong to wait."

"You busy tonight?"

"No. What'd you have in mind?"

"Playing gin, at the gallery while Clare hangs her show."

"Sure. It's such easy money."

6

At the gallery, we found three chairs and sat on two and played gin on the third while Clare and Ellie Bragg and a middle-aged man moved the old show out and Clare's photographs in. At eleven they quit and I paid Andy sixty dollars. Clare said nothing on the way back to the apartment or after we got there, except to say goodnight to Andy and to tell me that she had to return at ten in the morning.

I left her to herself in the bedroom and found Catherine in the kitchen where she'd been making bread. She did that when she was feeling the need to de-stress. Eight warm loaves were lined up on racks on the long counter, and she allowed me to cut the end off one that was full of nuts and seeds and little bits of fruit, and I munched on it and felt special.

I watched her wipe down the counter one last time and reach for a hand towel. I said, "I'm thinking about quitting."

"Quitting what?"

"The business. The playing."

Her eyebrows went up but she said nothing, just went on wiping her hands.

"You look like you don't believe me."

"I'm not sure I do. Have you told the others?"

"Paul and Philip."

"What did they say?"

I shrugged. "Philip didn't like it, but he won't try to stop me. Paul pissed in his pants and tried to bull me out of it. Andy'll be okay. Uncle Nick?" I shrugged again. "He surprises me sometimes. What the hell? What *can* they say? What do *you* say? What about the money?"

"Philip said a third of the money last year was from you."

"And you need the money."

"No. No, we live on what I make, and the rents."

"But you put all the money from the business into a trust for the kids. For college."

She nodded.

Then she said, "You do what you want. What you need. What *she* needs. I mean it."

"Yeah. What she needs." I kissed her cheek. "I'm going to bed."

7

Clare was still silent, just lying under the covers staring at the ceiling. I could damn near see her quivering. I showered and put on a pair of pajama pants, which I wore for the sake of the kids, and she still said nothing.

Until we were in bed together. Then she pushed my hand away from her breast and said, "They're going to hate it. No, they won't even do that. They'll think it's dumb."

"Who?"

"Everyone."

"Do you want some aspirin or something?"

"Oh, right, just take drugs."

"Alcohol, then? I have some whisky in my desk."

"All right."

I got a bottle and a small glass from my desk drawer, brought the water glass from my bathroom, and sat cross-legged on the bed with her and poured whisky. I took the bigger glass, she got the little glass.

She sipped it gingerly. "Actually, I hate whisky."

"I know. Do you want something else from the other room?"

"No, don't leave me alone here."

I raised my eyes to the heavens. "Then toss it off, stop sipping."

She did and shuddered and swallowed several times.

"Keep it down, damn it. Do you want some water?"

She bobbed her head wordlessly and I drank off the whisky in the water glass and brought it to her full of water.

"How do you drink that all the time?" she asked when she could finally speak.

I picked up the small glass she had abandoned, filled it, capped the bottle, and leaned on the desk. "I like it."

"Do you drink very much? Here, in your room, alone?"

"You know how much I drink."

"When you're with me." She fell back onto the pillows. "I want to photograph you like that," she said. "You look like a revolutionary."

That made me laugh.

"I want—I want to let myself sink into that strength—but I am so afraid that it would be a mistake. That I don't know how to make it work."

I resisted moving over to the bed, to her.

"Maybe nobody does before they try," I said.

"And I think maybe there is so much I don't know about you. I thought I did but I don't. My God, I thought your family were—were—I don't know! These shadowy beings who had their claws in you! How wrong could I be! I didn't know anything about you!"

"Ask me."

"Do you love me?"

"Ask me another."

"I tell you that I love you." I could hear the whisky in her voice. And maybe tears.

"Yes, you do."

"And don't you like it that I do?"

"Like it? Hearing you say it, seeing that look on your face gives me feelings I thought you had to die and go to heaven for."

"Then don't I get to have those feelings, too?"

"I am never ever giving you whisky again."

"Oh, you think this is just the whisky talking."

"You know how I feel about you and what you mean to me."

"Do *you* know?"

"I could just open my mouth and say it and what would it mean to either one of us? I still wouldn't know if the word meant what I feel. No. I won't say it and you can stop talking about it."

"So what I said was just cheap sentimentality?"

"No, that's different. You're different." I moved to the bed. "You need some sleep. Let me show you my relaxation techniques."

WEDNESDAY, FEBRUARY 29

1

The next morning the whisky had worn off and she was alternately edgy and silent. I got irritable and told her I wouldn't let her out of the apartment until she ate something, and she could see that I was prepared to be rougher than she was prepared to deal with, and she sullenly ate toast and drank juice.

The guards were on duty when I dropped her at the gallery and I breathed a sigh of relief as she went in the door. Feeling almost as edgy as she was, I went to the gym to jump rope, lift weights, and hit the speed bag with my left hand. The trainer made a few pointed remarks about my still evident cuts and bruises. At eleven Andy intercepted me just as I was leaving the locker room.

"A collection job," he said.

"Today? Can't it wait?"

"Paul says today."

"Paul can just go fuck himself." I shrugged into my jacket.

"Uncle Nick says do it. Come on, let's just get it over with. I have a lunch date."

We were in the stainless steel and glass lobby of a new downtown office tower and I was pushing the elevator button when Andy shivered violently.

"I hate these jobs," he said, more savagely than I'd ever heard from him.

We stepped into the elevator.

"Good," I said. "Let me know when you start liking it, so I can stay away from you."

On the fifteenth floor we entered the stylish reception room of an advertising agency and approached the desk. The extremely fashionable thirtyish brunette behind it watched us come with some interest, but backed her chair up two inches when we didn't stop until we were both right in front of her. She smiled, but neither of us returned it.

"Mr. Peterson," I said.

"Bob Peterson or—"

"Yes."

"May I tell him who's calling?"

"His physical therapist."

Andy made a slight appreciative sound next to me and turned away to admire the decor while I watched the woman relay my message. After three or four minutes Peterson came into the reception room, a middle-aged ex-journalist, probably ex-hockey player, running to fat. He frowned at us, and muttered an invitation to his office, a small cluttered inner room holding a computer and several tons of paper and magazines in loose stacks.

He stood behind the desk and the two of us stood in front of it.

"I suppose you're here about the money," he said, looking at his desk top. He put his hands in his pants pockets and jingled his change and keys.

I said, "Right. Forty-seven hundred dollars."

"Right, right. I meant to see you yesterday, you know, but I got held up. A meeting. Didn't get to the bank."

"Well," I said amiably, "we'll go there now."

"I'm pretty busy this morning." He took his hands out of his pockets and moved a stack of papers.

"It won't take long."

"Well, how about if I give you a check—"

"It's a bad check we're covering here, Bob. Cash only."

Peterson looked at us. "Are you brothers?" he blurted.

"No, cousins."

"You could be twins." He reached for a topcoat that was thrown over the top of a filing cabinet. "Gambling debts aren't legally collectible, you know," he said as he pushed his arms into the coat.

"Really?" said Andy. "I think I've heard that." He flexed his fingers absent-mindedly, shifted his weight to his other foot.

"You were pretty friendly at the poker table," Peterson said to me. He seemed to be looking warily at my black eye and the rest of the cuts and bruises. "Now you come here—to my office, damn it—and do this tough-guy act—"

"No act," I said.

"All right, all right."

We went with the now-closed-mouthed Peterson to his bank, accepted forty-seven hundred dollars in cash with controlled thanks, and left him on a nearby street corner.

"Nice tough-guy act," Andy said.

"No act," I said. "He owed us."

"It's an act for me, and you know it. And I think it's an act for you. Or is your blood so much colder than mine?" I opened my mouth and he said, "No. Never mind. I don't really want the answer. Come and eat with me and Kori."

After a leisurely blood-warming lunch at a Thai restaurant, I went to the gallery to wait for Clare to finish.

She was ready to go at three, and I walked her to the car with my arm around her shoulders.

"You seem considerably calmer," I said. "I thought I might have to peel you off the ceiling."

"It's all over now, win or lose, the die is cast. I've crossed the Rubicon."

"I wish I had your flair for phrasemaking. When do you have to be back?"

"Six-thirty."

We heated soup in Catherine's kitchen and drank red wine with it. I had to coax her to take the first spoonful, but then she managed to get a reasonable amount into herself.

When she was dressed and ready to go, I couldn't stop looking at her. Her new dress was a short, shimmering, loose-fitting black silk slip with thin straps and a front cut low enough to show the swell of her breasts. Her legs were in sheer black silky hose and her feet in tall black flat-heeled boots. Her only jewelry was her sapphire ring.

I said, "There is no more beautiful woman than you, anywhere."

She blushed pink. "I only want to look good enough to go out with you. I adore you in your headwaiter suit. And the black eye adds such a touch of elegance."

2

Her opening was one of twenty-odd openings, all in the neighborhood and all on the same night. At six-thirty there were already early-comers being let in the doors that were supposed to open at seven; by seven-thirty the small gallery was crowded. By eight-thirty it was packed.

I stood where she could find me just by moving her left hand. She said later that her clearest memories of the evening were the faces of the family in the crowd and the rest of it was mostly a blur of compliments and questions and faces, lights and smoke and noise. I heard her say quietly to about a dozen people that she would really like to photograph them and would they call her.

By ten almost everyone had left or had been politely urged out and at ten-thirty I took her away, even though a few stragglers remained. I walked her two blocks down the street to a bar I knew with comfortable high-backed booths. She was in a happy dreamy trance. Maybe I was too. We sat with our shoulders touching and drank white wine, and if we turned our heads, our lips would meet.

We were jerked out of the dream by two men in dark suits sliding into the booth.

I sat up straight and fast. "You're trespassing," I said in a hard voice. "Get out."

"Back down, Zandros," said one of them. "We're here to invite you to a card game."

Son of a bitch. I knew him. It was Black's bodyguard. Hugh Black from the poker game at Weiss's. Carl.

"No, thanks. Beat it. Now."

"My boss wants to talk to you, maybe play some cards. Miss Russell is also invited."

"Miss Russell doesn't play cards."

"I understand Miss Russell had some damage recently." He was very blond. His smooth, pale, good-looking face was entirely without expression. He lit a cigarette, let his coat hang open so we could see a gun in a shoulder holster. Clare shrank against me. I put my hand over hers.

I wasn't carrying a gun. I'd thought about it, about Finny, but I didn't want to scare Clare or embarrass her. Or explain it to her.

"Mr. Black wants to talk about how to prevent more damage."

"All right, I'll talk to him. He doesn't need to see Miss Russell."

"She comes along."

"And if we say no?"

He didn't bother to answer, just stood and waited.

With Clare there, I had no choice. These guys were not thugs but I figured them for twice as dangerous as every thug I'd ever known. I got to my feet and gave her a hand sliding out of the booth, keeping myself between her and the men. I helped her into her new coat and put my arm around her to walk out through the bar.

It was raining slightly, and we waited just outside the entrance while the man who hadn't said anything opened the door of a large dark car that was parked at the curb right in front. The non-talker drove, the talker sat in the back seat with me and Clare. She was in the middle and she sat up against me and held onto my coat with both of her hands and shivered.

"Clare," I muttered, "try to breathe at least."

"What's going on?" she whispered.

"I'm not sure, but don't fall apart on me."

"I'll try. But I'm afraid."

"That's okay. Just keep breathing."

3

They drove us to a large expensive suburban house in an expensive suburban neighborhood, and in an oatmeal-colored living room we were met by Hugh Black. He said, "Mr. Zandros. Good to see you again." Neither of us offered to shake hands. "Please sit down, Miss Russell," he said. "My name is Hugh Black." He was looking at her with a slight frown.

I guided her into a chair and stood next to her with a hand on her shoulder. She was watching him intently, staring at his face.

"Drink?" asked Black.

"No," I said.

Black splashed Martell XO into a glass and drank it down and poured more.

"Sam Zandros," he said. "I made you an offer in L.A. Did you think about it?"

"Not really."

"But you haven't said no. So I'm making it again, here and now."

"And if I say no?"

He drank off his Cognac. "Miss Frances Russell, the photographer, loses her eyesight in an accident."

Clare made a noise and started to rise and I pushed her back down.

I said, "Did you pay Barry Salter and some crony of his to wreck Miss Russell's apartment?"

She gave me a startled look.

He hesitated for the first time. Finally he said, "Yes."

A minute passed while I tried to size him up. I said, "If I do it?"

"That's it. Nothing else. You don't know it, but my word is good. When I get what I want."

I said, "You have the cards."

A tall young blond woman in a long dress came into the room. I knew her slightly. Her name was Cora. She smiled at me and sat down on a couch, striking a pose.

"So I do," said Black, ignoring Cora. "Shall we shake hands on it?"

I didn't move. "My word is good," I said.

"And you'll talk to your brothers?"

"I gave my word. They're in."

He said, "I'll make sure. Two of my men will meet you at your office tomorrow at noon."

I felt my temper rising and swallowed it. "If you insist."

"In the meantime, Miss Russell will be our guest."

"No," I said. "That's not necessary." I was entering the red zone.

Clare was frozen, speechless.

"I think it is," he said.

Carl took his gun from inside his jacket. It slipped out like it was greased. He'd done this before.

Black said, "No one's going to shoot you. If you make a move, Carl here will take out Miss Russell."

Carl moved quickly forward until his gun was against Clare's head.

Black said, "Back up, Zandros."

I backed up.

Cora was smiling.

Carl took Clare's arm, and pulled her to her feet. A fourth man, another underling, came into the room.

"She won't be hurt," said Black. "She won't be injured in any way. Not in any way. She'll be delivered tomorrow afternoon, after your meeting."

Clare was staring at me, shocked and white, and all I could do was look at her. One of the other men, the last to enter, came forward, pulled her coat off one arm, and held her wrist behind her back. He had a hypodermic syringe in one hand and he removed the cover on the needle with his teeth and jabbed the needle into Clare's bare arm. She said, "Sam," desperately, urgently, and I held her eyes with mine until hers rolled back and her lids fluttered and closed and she went limp. The one named Carl caught her and carried her out of the room. I breathed again.

Black lit a cigar. "Some friends of mine are here to play cards. Perhaps you'll join us? We can break in our agreement." He opened a drawer, took out two bundles of new hundreds still in bank wrappers—five thousand each—and handed them to one of the other men who handed them to me.

Black said, "That should start you out."

I glanced at the money and stuffed it into my pocket. "Where do we play?" I asked him.

4

He showed me to a card room—more oatmeal decor—down a hallway and up some steps. There were four men there, already playing, who all greeted us pleasantly. I'd played with one and heard of one other.

I was angry enough to play even more aggressively than I usually did. Their stacks of chips when I started looked almost even. By four-thirty I had eighty thousand dollars and the guests called it quits. Their stacks were hardly stacks at all. Black took his ten and thirty-five, and I pocketed the other thirty-five. It was high-class play, up a level from where I usually played, and it was exciting and easy to like.

"You do that so nicely," Black said. "No wonder they come back for more, just to see it done so well."

I gave Black a speculative look. "And what if I didn't do it at all? For you or anyone else."

Black was lighting another cigar. He shrugged. "No one who plays like you do can give it up. It's like it's your art."

I stared at him.

Black's tone was almost defensive. "I'm interested in things that are the best. People who do them the best."

After a moment I said, "I want to see her."

"Of course." He puffed a couple of times. "She won't be touched or hurt in any way. My word on it."

Carl led me to a pink bedroom in another part of the house, another level up. She was on her back in a large bed, under a puffy pink comforter. Her boots were on the floor by the bed and her coat on a chair next to it. There was a lamp on across the room. I lifted the comforter and saw that she was still in her dress and stockings. She was laid out neatly and comfortably, arms at her side, a pillow under her head.

Carl said, "No touching."

I said, "Fuck off, Carl."

She was breathing easily. I put my fingers on the pulse in her neck. It was strong and steady. I put my hand on her cheek for a few seconds, and turned away. I stood and looked at Carl.

"You'll be here?" I asked.

He nodded.

"He's your boss?"

He nodded again.

Cora was sitting on a couch near the front door, a coat over her long dress. She had been in and out of the card room most of the night, until Black told her to go somewhere and sit down.

"I guess you need a ride home, Sam," she said.

I looked at her for a moment. "I guess I do."

She had a small noisy car and she drove it fast and badly.

"I haven't seen you lately," she said.

"I been busy."

She lived in a six-story brick block on the wrong side of downtown. She drove into the small parking lot next to the building, and we both got out. I started for the street.

"Wait!" she said. "Wait! Don't you want to stay?"

"You must be joking," I said over my shoulder.

"Don't you like me?" she said.

I yelled back, "You're a whore, lady. Nobody likes you."

"He already paid," she called.

I kept going.

THURSDAY, MARCH 1

1

I walked to Andy's apartment where I took a long shower and borrowed some clothes. Over coffee and toast and peanut butter in his tiny kitchen I told him the whole story.

He yawned and scratched his chest, bare under his robe. "I'd like to know where Kevvy Smith sits in this."

"Yeah. Nice of you not to say I told you so."

"Doesn't apply. Nothing she knew or didn't know could have made any difference."

I poured more coffee for both of us. "I never played for anyone outside the family."

"None of us have."

"Guess I've never been strong-armed before, either."

He said, "What he says he'll take and that's all—do you trust him?"

"Yeah, oddly enough, I do."

"Can you swallow your pride for her?"

I said, "I will do anything for her."

"We're okay then." He put his arm around my shoulders and squeezed. He stood and put the dirty dishes into the sink.

I said, "I told Philip and Paul I was thinking of quitting."

Andy whistled through his teeth. "And Paul pissed his pants, right?"

"It'd be worth quitting just to see him sweat. But I guess that's no longer on the table."

He just said, "Yeah."

We walked to the office. Philip, Paul, and Uncle Nick were all there, and I told the story again.

They were quiet when I finished.

"Nothing else you could do," Philip said finally. "You call it. Whatever you say."

Uncle Nick nodded. "If the young woman—"

I said, "Clare. Her name is Clare."

Uncle Nick said, "Of course. Clare. I'm sorry. If Clare is unhurt, we go with your agreement."

I said, "If she's touched, I kill Black."

No one said anything. Was that yes or no? I didn't know. I didn't care.

Paul just said nothing. Unusual for him.

Andy and I played gin on a corner of the table, Philip entered numbers on the computer, Uncle Nick read the sporting newspapers, and Paul picked at his fingernails and read the sports pages in the daily paper.

Finally Paul said, "Sam."

"Not now."

"Does this mean—"

Andy said, "Gin."

"Sam—"

I said, "Fuck."

Paul said, "You'll be playing for us now, right? I mean, you play for Black, you might as well play for us, right. Fuck the I-quit shit?"

I leaned back in my chair and turned and looked straight at Paul.

He said, "This Black could put us in touch with some big money. Opportunity knocking."

"Fucking parasite," I said.

"The fuck does that mean? Me? You mean me? Listen, I work here—"

"You suck blood here. You talk on the phone here and bring your whores here and act the man here and you'd walk over the dead bodies of everyone in the room for a buck."

"And what about fucking Catherine? She doesn't play and she gets her share."

Andy clamped his hand around my wrist.

Uncle Nick gave Paul a shocked look. Philip sucked in his breath.

"At least I play—" Paul said in an injured, whiny tone.

"And lose," I said, not keeping the disgust from my voice.

"Enough," said Uncle Nick.

Paul said, "I've got more to say—"

I said, "You've got fuck all to say."

Uncle Nick said, "Enough! This is for later. When she—when Clare is back."

Paul went back to picking his fingernails, and Andy and I played gin until eleven, then Andy paid me seventy-five dollars and went downstairs for sandwiches.

Carl and another of Black's men arrived at noon, and the rest of us deferred to Uncle Nick, who smoked a cigar and was openly contemptuous.

"Sam gave his word and that was good for all of us. Your boss didn't need to drag a woman into it."

"You understand the terms," Carl persisted.

"Of course we understand. Now let the girl go."

"She's in the car."

Andy and I followed him down to the street. The same big car was at the curb, and I jerked open the back door. Clare was slumped in the other corner, her coat tossed over her. Her hair was disheveled and she looked exhausted. Her eyes were open. I climbed into the car and reached for her. She struggled to sit up and I helped her and she leaned against me. I held her.

"Are they gone?" she asked hoarsely.

"In a minute. Soon as we get out of this car."

"Let's get out."

I helped her to the sidewalk and the car drove away. "Are you all right?" I asked. "Did they hurt you? Touch you?"

"No. Nothing like that." She seemed content to stand there, not moving, my arms around her but not holding her up. "They scared me."

"Yeah, they're scary guys. What do you remember?"

"Going there. And that man—Mr. Black—telling you that you have to play for them or—" She stopped and took a breath. "And you said you would."

"Right."

"Then he said I had to stay there and the other one had a gun and then they both were holding me and there was that woman—you knew her—"

"Yeah."

"Your eyes held me up and then I fell down."

"And that's all. It's all over."

"All over?"

"Yes. Absolutely."

"They won't—"

"No, they won't do anything."

"That's what he said." Then, "You're here."

"I'm here."

She sighed deeply and leaned against me. "I was so scared," she said.

"Jesus, Clare. I'm so sorry!"

"It wasn't your fault—"

Maybe it wasn't, maybe it was.

"But I thought—" She choked on the words.

"What?"

"I thought they were killing me!"

2

I paced Catherine's kitchen, a glass of wine in one hand, gesturing with the other. I was furious beyond anything I'd ever felt before. Andy was leaning against a counter, also drinking wine, and listening.

"She thought they were killing her. And I was standing there, watching them do it. It was going to be the last thing she ever saw, the last picture, me standing there watching them kill her."

Andy shrugged. "You didn't have a lot of choices, man. Not like you would if you were, say, Captain Marvel."

"Right. There was nothing I could do. I know that, you know that. But I should have done something. We know that, too."

Friday, March 2

1

A little after eight the next morning she opened her eyes and saw me watching her. We were in my bed, and I had been watching her for almost an hour.

"What day is it?" she asked.

"Friday."

"I missed Thursday." She had slept all afternoon and night after I'd gotten her back to Catherine's.

"You wouldn't have liked it."

After a couple of minutes she said, "I'm hungry."

2

We showered, separately, and dressed and went to the kitchen. I ate Grape Nuts with a sliced banana and we both watched Catherine cook and I watched Clare eat eggs and toast, then I poured coffee for us both and finally she looked at me.

"I'm going home today," she said.

So that was it. "You can't. There's nothing there."

"Well, I'm going anyway."

"Don't be silly."

"Oh, just because it's not up to you, it's silly."

"Even if I had thought of it, it would be silly."

"Well, I'm going."

Catherine said, "I can lend you some things."

I said, "Whose side are you on?" and Clare said, "You don't have to do that."

"You'll need some things. Sam, there are some boxes in the store-room. Would you bring them up?"

I left the kitchen. I didn't even slam the door.

3

I stood in my room, watching her again, watching her gather her things together. Every now and then she shot me a sideways glance. If she was reading my face, she was reading one hell of a lot of anger and frustration.

"Are you really going to do this?" I asked finally.

"You know I am."

I considered throwing my coffee cup across the room and set it carefully on my desk. "You need a bed to sleep on."

"Catherine is lending me some blankets and pillows and Stephen's air mattress."

"You're planning to spread blankets on the floor and sleep on an air mattress? Well, I'm not."

She refolded a shirt. "You don't come into it."

"What does that mean?"

She sat down suddenly on my desk chair. "I had breakfast with Mr. Black. When was it, yesterday?"

"Yeah. Yesterday."

"He offered me breakfast, anyway. I didn't have much appetite."

"Right."

"He said you agreed to let him stake you in card games. Poker. That you'd play for him, with his money, and you'd get a share."

"I will. I already did."

"He apologized to me."

"Did he."

"He offered me a bunch of money. Buy new cameras, everything."

"You turned him down."

"Yes." She picked up her new silk blouse, started to fold it, then crumpled it into a ball and shoved it into the box. "I said I didn't want to be beholden to him."

"You said beholden?"

"It's a word."

"Right."

"He paid Barry to wreck my things."

"Yeah, I'd figured out that much."

"When?"

"After a guy named Kevvy Smith called me. The day after it happened. I didn't know it was Black, but I knew what he was."

"While I still thought that it was between Barry and me. And you let me think that. You *let* me think that. For my own good, I suppose."

I didn't answer.

She said hotly, "You let me be a fool, Sam. You treated me like a fool and you let me be one. Everyone else knew and I was the dummy in the middle."

"You're not a fool."

She looked away, stared out the window. "You *let* me think that." Her hands were fists on the windowsill. "It *wasn't* me that someone was after, it was you. I was just a *thing* to get you with. He said it was a warning. I was a warning. And I thought you went to beat someone up because of me. Like you said, a champion."

"Clare, please don't. I thought—"

"Mr. Black will leave me alone now. He said so. And he said that everyone else will leave me alone. That he'll see to that. And I guess he can. He said he doesn't need me anymore. Because you'll be doing what he wants." A pause. "I was right about getting mixed up with families." Another pause. "Why couldn't it just be the way it was before?"

"You know why."

"I need to be by myself for a while."

"You don't want to see me?"

My voice was hoarse and she looked up and looked quickly away. She said, "You say you want to marry me but you won't—"

"Won't what?"

"Just what is it you want to marry?" She shook her head. "I need to figure this out and I can't think straight when you're around."

"For how long?"

"I don't know."

"Maybe forever?"

Her body jerked like I'd hit her, and maybe I had. She shook her head, but she didn't speak.

I dug into my pocket for my keys, took her door key from the ring, put the key on the desk, and left the room. I was gone from the apartment when she came out.

From the park across the street I watched Catherine and one of the security guys help her load her boxes into her car and watched her drive off. I decided to go to work. I walked to the office and spent the rest of the day and evening taking phone calls. Nobody said boo to me and I guessed Catherine had called Philip. And what would Clare think of *that*?

Then I spent half the night walking, half hoping some asshole would front me. No luck.

SATURDAY, MARCH 3

I called Harry and met him at a little bar called 49.

We ordered beers and he said, almost gently, "I heard."

I said, "Jesus, how? From whom?"

"I got a call from your cousin Andy."

"I didn't know you were on calling terms with Andy."

"We've played in a few games together."

"I'm starting to think Clare knows what she's talking about."

He flashed his very white teeth in a grin. "Don't you doubt that lady. She may be getting messages from the elves and faeries, but she's one shrewd lass."

"Okay, let me tell you the whole story."

He nodded and I did, everything. We finished our second beers just as I finished my story, and I waved at the waitress and gestured for two more.

He said, "I heard Kevvy Smith was being pushed. But I never heard of this Hugh Black before."

"Nor had we. But Kevvy Smith complained about somebody from Chicago, and I guess that's Black's home field."

He said, "Toddlin' town, my home town. Although we considered Chicago a suburb of Bridgeport. My prediction is that Kevvy Smith will lose this one."

The beers came.

I said, "I want a favor."

"I think I might be able to accommodate you."

"Good. I want a spy."

"To spy on Clare."

"Right."

He gave me a narrow-eyed look. "Stalking is against the law."

"Like you'd care. Anyway, forget the night-vision binoculars. That's not what I'm asking for. I just want to know how she's doing. What she's doing."

He drank beer and frowned. "I reserve the right to censor what I tell you."

"Right. That's up to you."

"You know, she and I have been friends a long time. I think she trusts me."

"Damn it, I'm not asking you to betray her trust. Just tell me what she's doing. Does she need anything. Is anybody hassling her. I'll be out of town more, again, and I want her safe while I'm gone."

"Okay. I can do that. Don't call us, we'll call you."

"Right."

THURSDAY, MARCH 8

Black called and said he wanted to set up a game on Saturday night in Kansas City. I almost thought he'd forgotten me.

"Eight players," he said, "including you. Do you want to know who they are? What they do?"

"Any of them pros?"

"Not this time."

"Where is it?"

"Private club. They call it the Kansas Club. Carl will do security and I hire a pro dealer."

"Dress code?"

"Coat and tie."

"Who pays my expenses?"

"I do. But I don't pay for girls. There might be some freebies."

"Bail?"

"That will not be a problem. I'll make a reservation for you at the Nickerson Hotel. The club is on the top floor. Carl will email your ticket this afternoon. A car will be at the KC airport for you. I'll meet you there for dinner on Saturday, seven-thirty."

You got to eat, right? Why not eat with a crime boss?

SATURDAY, MARCH 10

S o this was the big time. Not too different, actually, from my travels as a lesser mortal. Only the money was different.

The plane ride was in first class, the car and driver were there as promised, the Nickerson was posh Victorian decor, and under the retro surface, very up to date.

The room was comfortable. Well lit, nicely decorated, all the amenities. But it was just another hotel room. And I was goddamn tired of hotel rooms. I'd been liking staying home a lot the last few months. I hoped that Black didn't have in mind a game every weekend. And how much say would I have in it? Would my options include no? Was I the dog or the pony? Did it matter?

I asked the bellman to bring me a six-pack of tonic water, then found the room's refrigerator in the dressing room that adjoined the bath. I'd had a beer on the plane, but I wouldn't drink any alcohol again until after the game. There was a steamer device in the dressing room to freshen my jacket and trousers. There was also a hair dryer, and I wondered if anyone ever mixed them up. I poured tonic water into a drinking glass and added some ice. My mouth was dry—from the dry air in the plane, I told myself. I had time for a nice nap and another bottle of tonic water.

Black called up from the front desk at seven-fifteen and I went down to meet him. He had on a black suit and tie and a white dress shirt and he looked like a high-school principal. I had on dark-blue Dockers, a dark-blue wool sport coat, beige shirt, and a rep tie with red and blue stripes—colors of some school I'd never attended.

We ate dinner in the hotel's dining room. I'd learned long ago to eat carefully and lightly before an important game. I had two very nice pan-fried catfish filets and a spinach salad and some crispy fried shoestring potatoes. For dessert, a scoop of orange sherbet. I drank soda water.

Black asked me a number of questions about my family. He actually seemed interested. Then he asked after Clare.

I said, "We're no longer seeing each other, but I know she's—all right."

He looked almost self-conscious. "Because of my activities?"

I said, "Only partly. I was stupid."

He said, "Is there anything—"

I said, "No," perhaps a bit sharply.

He nodded.

After that we talked about, of all things, the Civil War. I had majored in history and was still interested, and Black apparently was a reader. Being in Missouri in a city called Kansas, we discussed Ellis Hamhill's new book on Quantrill's Raiders, which we had both read, then talked about guerrillas in general. After dinner we went to sit in the bar, where we smoked cigars—he had some very good Cubans—and he drank brandy and I drank more soda water. At eight-thirty Carl came into the bar.

Black said, "You haven't really met Carl, have you? Carl Huxley."

Carl nodded, bent forward slightly and said to Black, "Mr. Portman is here."

"Ask him to join us."

And so it began.

Sunday, March 11

I flew back to St. Paul with slightly over five grand in my pocket. I'd walked out of that room feeling a great relief, and now I was feeling well pleased with myself. I'd played with the big boys and won, and I had wire-transferred one hundred sixty-two thousand, courtesy of the hotel's private bank, to St. Paul. My money got there ahead of me by several hours.

Back home I took a cab to Catherine's, showered and changed clothes, called Philip to tell him I was back and to tell Cy about the money, and called Harry. We met at a hotel near the office. The Redstone. It was sort of shabby as a hotel but the coffee shop was open twenty-four seven, they served breakfast twenty-four seven, and the food, which was both American and Asian, was top notch both east and west. Harry ordered a club sandwich and I ordered won ton soup and imperial egg rolls. I had had a huge breakfast after we finished playing at six o'clock, and had slept on the plane.

"Good game?" he asked.

"Yeah. Tell me about Clare."

He sighed. "They don't write, they don't call, and then, when I finally see him, it's tell me about Clare."

I said, "Hello, I'm fine, I won, how are you, tell me about Clare."

"Dropped in unheralded at her apartment—"

"Was it okay? They were supposed to clean it."

"It was squeaky clean and very empty. Her living room furnishings are three wooden chairs and her old desk. I used the bathroom and got a look at her bedroom. Did they even destroy all her furniture?"

"Axe," I said. "And knives."

I leaned back in the booth, my hands wrapped around a mug of tea.

He said, "She's living out of boxes—clean boxes but boxes—and sleeping on a new futon. She caught me looking and said that for two nights she'd slept on a blanket and an air mattress that kept collapsing and it was not only hard but cold. I said did they get everything and she showed me around. She got an advance from the insurance people and bought four wooden chairs, one for her studio, and the futon. She went to estate sales and bought stuff for her kitchen. And she bought a camera and a tripod and a couple of lights and those umbrella things and stuff for her darkroom. She says that this week she's painting the studio. I offered to help, so I'm going over there tomorrow afternoon. And we're going to do a smudge before we paint."

"Good. Stay off the futon."

Harry grinned. "I love that woman but I've met one I think I want for my own."

"You should have seen that place. It didn't look like anyone could ever live there again."

"She's doing it."

I said, "She works fast."

"Yeah, it looks like someone lives there, but maybe only part-time."

"Does she need money?"

He said, "You know, I don't think there's anything you could do that would hurt her more at this point."

I didn't answer him for a while, just concentrated on my tea. "Let me know if she does," I said. "I can maybe talk to the claims agent. He can find an act-of-god clause or something."

Our food came.

He said, "Or act of Greek."

I said, "Same thing."

"And I have a message for you. She said, 'I know you see Sam. Tell him she stole my ring.'"

"She?"

"Yeah. Definitely said she."

I thought back and remembered Clare at the gallery and holding her hand and feeling the ring on her finger.

"Okay, I'll take care of it. Tell me about your woman."

"Karen Lund. She's a librarian."

"Somebody's got to do it," I said carelessly.

"Do what, exactly?" He suddenly had that look that said he'd as soon kill you as not.

"Keep Western Civilization together. A thankless task."

"Yeah." He was mollified. "She works at the U. She speaks eight languages. Her birth language was Norwegian. She's just tall enough and just round enough and she has copper-colored hair and amber-colored eyes and just the right number of freckles. And a cute little birthmark that you are never going to see."

"I don't poach."

"I know. Tell me about the game."

FRIDAY, MARCH 16

1

Black had set up another game, this time in St. Louis, for Saturday night. Same format. Meeting room on the top floor of a big hotel. First class all the way.

I was in the kitchen telling Catherine when I'd be leaving and when returning, and she said, "I saw Clare."

"Where?"

"At her apartment. I went to visit her."

"How did that happen?"

"I called her and invited myself. I took her a loaf of bread."

"How is she?"

"I think she's doing—I was going to say fine but I don't think that's accurate. And well is not the right word either."

I said impatiently, "On a scale of one to ten."

She laughed softly. "A six."

"That's all?"

"Sam, sometimes you are an idiot."

"Yes, well, give me some details."

"She showed me a big camera that she'd bought used—she said it was the only way these days and on her budget to get what she really wanted—and several other items of photographic equipment that were utter mysteries to me. But Ioulia was with me and she was fascinated, and it was a joy to see Ioulia fascinated by something other than clothes and makeup."

"Girls will be girls."

"Anyway, she told me she's back in business. She got a list of interested people from the woman who runs that gallery and she's been calling them. She says when she first started her studio she had to have another job, but not this time."

"She's calling people? She hates that."

"So she said. But she's doing it. She's doing what she needs to do. And you leave her alone and stay out of it."

"She said that?"

"No, I say that. If you ever want her back, you leave her alone."

2

Was it better to think about her or not think about her? The pain that roweled through me when I thought about her never lessened and the sickening, breath-stealing absence of her never filled up.

SATURDAY, MARCH 17

Black and I had dinner again, and when we sat down, I said, "Here's something I want to get out of the way before I start eating." I shook out my napkin. "I got a message. From Clare Russell, through a trusted friend. The message was, she stole my ring."

"'She stole my ring.'"

"Right." I took a piece of paper from the inside pocket of my jacket. "This is a picture of it. I gave it to her, for Christmas. It's an antique. As you can see, a carved gold band and a sapphire. Not fake. She was wearing it the night—"

"Yes. I'll take care of it. May I borrow the picture?"

"You can keep it. It's a printout and I have the file."

"Computer talk. I can't decide if I'm too old for that or not."

I said, "I don't believe it's an age thing. I think it's a need thing."

We discussed it all through dinner.

MONDAY, MARCH 19

1

On Sunday I came back from St. Louis late in the afternoon with just over one hundred twenty grand. I'd wire-transferred all of it, but to my own account. On Monday I went to the office early enough that I could give odds Uncle Nick and Philip and maybe Andy would be there but not Paul. I was right.

Philip said, "How are you?" and gave me a questioning look.

I laughed. "Don't worry. I won. One twenty." Andy and I bumped fists. "But I need to talk to you three and not Paul."

Philip said, "He's still family."

"Right. So's a kidney stone. I want to hold back some of this money. I figure half to hold back and half to the business."

Andy said, "For Clare?"

"Some for Clare, some for all the kids. Mainly I want to cover Clare and Nicky outside the regular accounts, without singling him out. And I don't want it available to Paul or Lillian."

Philip said, "To do that, you'll have to make it unavailable to all of us, I think."

"Then I will."

Uncle Nick said, "Give it to Cy. He'll take care of it."

I looked at Philip. He nodded.

2

Harry and I met at the Redstone again. He was wearing a rumpled old light-brown corduroy sport coat that he wore a lot when he played and that always looked like he'd been sleeping in it. He said it was his academic look. I said it was his academic disguise, as in, how could you take this guy seriously at the card table, discuss and show your work. Usually he wore it over a tatty T-shirt from one or another rock concert. But today he was wearing what looked like a crisp new shirt. A real shirt, oxford cloth, with buttons down the front, and a button-down collar. Thin red stripes on beige.

"Is that a new shirt?" I demanded.

He smiled, smugly I thought. "My lady gave it to me."

"Karen?"

"Uh huh."

"When do I get to meet a woman who got you into a new shirt? With a collar. Jesus."

"Soon. But today she's busy having fun with your lady. And later we will be helping that same lady to finish painting her apartment. And hang pictures."

I was jealous. I wanted to hang pictures for Clare.

I said, "Where are these two virtuous women?"

"Thrift shopping. And taking Clare's bicycle to be fixed."

"Clare has a bicycle?"

"She just got it. At a garage sale. An old three-speed. A clunker. And a lovely shade of what I am informed is Nile green."

"What color is it really?"

"Ugly. Very ugly."

3

He gave me a ride back to the office.

"Been to Elmore's lately?" he asked.

The sports bar Clare and I had gone to on New Year's Day. And Harry had said, "Something's happened," and something had.

He said, "You should go by there. Take a look at the art."

Art? At Elmore's?

4

I worked at the office for a while and then went out for an afternoon beer at Elmore's. I got a glass of Summit EPA at the tap, and looked at pictures. They were all from New Year's Day, black and white, blown up almost to poster size, matted in pristine white, and scattered among signs advertising vodka and beer and a meat raffle. Each one had a little card next to it with a number identifying the photo—there were thirty all told—and her name—Frances Russell—and an invitation to consult the bartender about how to purchase the photo. Good. At least she hadn't spread her phone number all over Elmore's. Sixteen of them had little red cards attached that said SOLD.

I'd seen some of them before, on the worktable at her apartment or on her wall, but not all of them. Most of them were headshots. I recognized maybe a third of them. The ones I knew, she'd nailed. I wandered from the front door down through the bar and around the back room and to the front again. The one closest to the front door, number one, was of Harry and me, half-turned into the room, leaning on the bar, waiting for our order, both looking somber. I wondered what we'd been talking about.

When I was done, I went over to put my empty glass on the bar. The bartender came down to get it and said, "You like those pictures? You're in one. They're for sale if you want to buy one."

"Yeah. What's she charging for them?"

"Thirty bucks."

She could hardly be making expenses.

"Selling well?"

"Yeah, real well."

I said, "How much does the bar get?"

"Nothing. Terry thinks it makes us look good."

"It does. And I want to buy number one. Pay you up front?"

"Yeah. Then I put the red card on it. She's closing the show on April fifteenth and you can pick it up after that."

Closing the show. Jesus. Next he'll be wearing a beret.

"Terry'll keep them in the office. He helped her pick out which ones. Here, write your name on here. She says, anyone throws a glass of beer at it, you get a new one."

"Terry's a patron of the arts now."

"Yeah, he's thinking nudes next."

"I'll just bet he is."

WEDNESDAY, MARCH 21

I finally met Karen Lund. The three of us were at Tomato Red for an early supper. Then Karen and Clare were going to a movie and Harry and I were going off to play. As we got settled into our chairs, Karen, who looked exactly as Harry had described her, with the additional aspect of being a formidable life force, said, "I know you're Harry's good friend, but I wasn't really sure I wanted to meet you." She had a very faint Norwegian accent. Actually she sounded almost British. I guessed it was Brits who'd taught her English.

I looked at her for a few seconds, then said, "As I understand it, if you find me contemptible, Harry won't be my friend for much longer."

She looked at Harry and turned bright red. He shrugged.

I said, looking at my menu, "Has Clare told you I'm a monster?"

"No, but she wouldn't, would she."

I said, "No."

Harry said, "Because you aren't."

The waiter came back. I ordered a tonic water and Harry ordered fizzy water. Karen said, "Am I the only one drinking beer?"

Harry said, "Yes," and she ordered a Bell's.

I said to the waiter, "Another minute with the menus?"

He said certainly and went away.

She said, "Are you both on the wagon?"

Harry said, "Only for the next twelve hours or so."

She looked at me. "I'm surprised."

Now I was surprised. "Why?"

"Well, someone told me that you're a—a heavy drinker."

I closed my menu and put it on the table. "Who?"

She looked at Harry. He was concentrating on his menu.

She said, "A woman spoke to me when Clare and I went shopping the other day. We were in a consignment shop on Grand. Clare was in the fitting room and this woman approached me." She took a deep breath. "She said is that Clare Russell I just saw you with and I said who are you and she said tell her she should stay away from Sam Zandros because he's a drunk, they all are, and sooner or later he'll be beating up on her. She said tell her that from a friend. And I said what friend and she said Lily and she left. I didn't tell Clare about her."

I blew out the breath I'd been holding.

Harry was back in the game. He said, "What did she look like?"

Karen said, "She was about forty-five, maybe a little less under the makeup. She had dark eyes and she wore a lot of dark eye makeup. And either her hair was bleached or she wore a wig. She was taller than I am and—well, everyone is—and she had a large—bosom."

I said, "Fat boobs or big boobs?"

She actually blushed again. "Big boobs."

I said, "Lillian."

Harry said, "Your brother Paul's wife."

"Uh huh."

He said, "I've never seen her."

"Well, that's what she looks like." I smiled at Karen. "Good description. But you shouldn't talk to strangers, girlie."

Harry said, "Clare knows better than that."

The waiter came back and hovered, so we ordered.

Karen folded her hands on the table and looked across at me and said, very serious, "Listen, I'm sorry. I listened to gossip and believed it on no grounds whatsoever. I didn't tell anybody, but—but I could have."

"But you didn't." I smiled at her some more. "Don't worry. In another hour you'll be loving me. Totally. Harry will be a fading memory."

"But you'll spurn me."

I patted her hand and said consolingly, "It'll be for the best."

She said coldly and loudly, "You son-of-a-bitch. Leading me on—How dare you!"

Bette Davis had never been colder.

Someone at another table looked at her and away quickly.

Harry started laughing and choked on his fizzy water. And all during dinner he kept looking at her in a way that said he was filled with wonder. I knew the feeling.

THURSDAY, MARCH 22

I went into the office early again because Paul rarely arrived before eleven. Everyone else was there. I told Uncle Nick and Philip and Andy about Karen Lund and Lillian. I said I didn't want to break the agreement our fathers and uncles made, but I've had it with playing to support him and his nasty little habits and his nasty wife. I said they better keep her away from me. I said that if either of them—Paul or Lillian—came within half a mile of Clare and I found out about it, I'd put my own version of a restraining order into play.

There was a very long silence. Then Uncle Nick said, "Let's have Cy figure out exactly what we have and how we can divide up the business. Whatever cash and investments we have now in the business, as of today. Then whatever we make from now on we put into new accounts, to wait until we decide what to do. And we keep this to ourselves."

I said, "Okay. I can live with that. For now. And my money through Black? I still want to divide some of it into the new accounts that Cy is setting up for me. Fifty-forty-ten. I get ten, the family gets forty."

Philip pressed his lips together and nodded his head wearily. Maybe even sadly. He was the only one in the family who'd ever been close to Paul. But that was mainly an age thing. He was too much of a realist to let this go now.

SATURDAY, MARCH 24

Another Saturday out of town. A brand new venue—Denver. I was getting accustomed to—maybe even actually liking—the flying in and out, everything taken care of and first-class all the way, and having dinner with Hugh Black before the game. He was an interesting man. He never gave away anything about his own history, but it was clear that he was a self-educated man. He had read widely but he didn't have that kind of roundedness of thought that comes from being tumbled with other minds in the academic cement mixer. But we had some very interesting conversations and I never toadied him. A couple of times I could see him burning but he hadn't shot me yet.

As we sat down, he handed me Clare's ring. I examined it closely. It was unharmed.

Black said, "I had it cleaned."

I said, "Thank you. I'll like getting it back to her and she'll like having it back."

He said, "I think my name doesn't need to come into it."

I said, "If you prefer."

I didn't ask how he'd gotten it. I didn't want to know.

I tucked it into my watch pocket.

His man Carl Huxley was always nearby. I had at the beginning wondered if he was the one who helped Salter and then knifed him, but I decided not. Carl was too fastidious. Always clean, neat, and well dressed. I couldn't see him swinging an axe. An idea came to me while we were eating dinner.

I said, "I want to ask a question. If this is completely out of bounds, just tell me."

"Go ahead."

"Do you have any of the kind of influence in the St. Paul Police Department that could get me copies of a couple of police reports?"

He chewed and swallowed. We were both eating steak, an indulgence for me before a game. But this was beef country. I had a very tasty little filet. He said, "Aren't they public?"

"I don't know. Maybe not the kind I want. And I'd as soon they didn't know I was looking."

"What do you want?"

"You remember Barry Salter?"

He looked disgusted, but all he said was, "Yes."

"He was killed with a knife."

He nodded.

"And so was a man named Gordy Terrell, who was found dead in Clare Russell's front hall last September."

Black said, "And you want to know if it was the same knife. And did anything else connect them."

"Yes."

"I think," he said slowly, "that I can get what you want." He ate another bite. "Why do you want to know?"

"There's a cop in St. Paul—just your middle-of-the-road cop but he would like very much to tag me for either Terrell or Salter or both. Or anything. It's an itch he can't scratch in polite company. I would like to get out from under and I would like Clare to be out of the running, no loose ends."

"I can fix this one for you."

"For real? I don't want to put some poor fish in my place just because I have a better insurance policy."

That was one of the times he didn't shoot me.

"For real," he said. "I can give the cop the guy he needs and the proof, and no one's conscience needs to be pricked."

"I'd owe you one."

"You're paying on the installment plan. Do you know if Miss Russell is all right?"

"Yes. She is. We have mutual friends."

"Good." A sip of water. "Good."

SUNDAY, MARCH 25

Sunday dinner was at Philip and Sofia's, and Paul and his family weren't there. Andy was there. Sofia and Catherine were in the kitchen, Meli and Ioulia had disappeared into Meli's room, Stephen was at the dining-room table working on his math, and Thomas and Jamie were between me and Andy on the sofa, trying not to wiggle or giggle. Both wiggling and giggling had been forbidden. Uncle Nick and Philip were in armchairs across from us. The conversation was about basketball teams and semifinals, which were in progress, and the profits accruing therefrom, and Philip was tracking three different sports channels on the big-screen TV. Uncle Cy was sometimes with us at Sunday dinner, but he and Peter and Mike were at the office. Philip and Andy and I would go in after dinner.

The doorbell buzzer went off and Philip went to answer it. We heard the security man's tinny voice in the intercom, then Philip speaking. We heard Philip open the front door and the quiet swish of the elevator doors. Then Philip's voice and then Paul's voice and Lillian's.

They came in and took off coats in the hallway, and Philip stepped into the living room and gestured to Jamie and told him to get his mother. Jamie ran to the kitchen and Thomas moved closer to me. I gave him a little hug and stood up.

"Time to go," I said to Andy.

He drank off the rest of his scotch and stood.

Sofia came out. "But I thought you were at your friends' today," she said to Lillian, while Philip helped with coats. And Paul didn't.

Lillian made a face and Paul said loudly, "They called and said they had to go to a dance recital. Folk dancing. His brother's kid. I ask you." He headed straight for the liquor.

Andy and I edged past Lillian and Young Nicky, who got a head pat from each of us, and took our jackets from the wall hooks. Andy said, "See you later, Philip. I'll call you." And we went out the door.

I headed for the stairs, too riled to wait for the elevator. In the car, while he waited a few minutes for the engine to warm up, Andy said, "She's a bitch and all, but are you taking this particular example of bitchery a bit too hard?"

"How the hell do I know how particular it is? She said that to a total stranger. What's she saying to anyone else?"

"Good point." He pulled out into the street.

"Damn right. I couldn't sit there in the same room with them. Either one of them. But you could go back. Have your dinner. Take Uncle Cy with you."

He said, "Nope. You Lone Ranger. Me faithful Indian companion."

"Do you think the Ranger and Tonto slept together?"

"Maybe."

TUESDAY, APRIL 3

Harry and Karen and I had dinner at Thai Thai Place by the U before he and I headed out to a game. I held out Clare's ring to him.

Karen said, "May I see it?" and I said sure and let her have it.

She examined it very closely. "It's lovely," she said. "And impressive. Antique, isn't it? Does it have a hidey for poison?"

I smiled. "No, it doesn't, Miss Borgia."

She said, "I presume the stone is real. You wouldn't give her fake."

"When Harry gives you baubles, does he let you eat the Cracker Jacks?"

Harry said, "Boy howdy, there goes my poker profits."

I said, "When you're an amateur, it's winnings. When you're a pro, it's profits. You have winnings."

Karen tried the ring on her finger and admired it, then took it off and handed it to Harry and gave him a big smile.

I said, "Give it back to her, will you? And tell her the finder had it cleaned."

"Sure."

Sunday, April 15

No game one week, but both Friday and Sunday nights the next, in Chicago. Stayed over Saturday. The hotel was the Clark, as usual. Found a gym where I could claim reciprocal privileges, caught a movie by myself, found a game not far from the hotel, in the back room of a tavern that also sold great sausages and excellent beer. And went to bed alone. I hadn't had sex since—well, since. Was I crazy?

Dinner with Hugh Black on Sunday.

He said, "Are you losing weight?"

I said, "I don't think so." In fact I had dropped about five pounds, which was not exactly surplus.

He smiled and said, "Don't get sick. I've been making a very nice profit on our venture."

I said, "I'd rather not talk about that, if you don't mind." Maybe my tone was harder than I meant, because he looked across the table with a sharp eye.

He said, "Then we won't," and he changed the subject to tell me about a guy in the game that night.

Then he said, "By the way, Sergeant Linden has just today arrested the killer of Barry Salter and Gordy Terrell. A young man from St. Paul named Finny Salter. Brother of Barry. Associate of the Smiths. Linden has plenty of evidence and it's good. Salter did it."

Finny Salter? Finny killed his brother?

"And you're turning him in for it."

He said, "He didn't kill anyone for me, if that's what you're imply-ing." Another time that he didn't shoot me. He chewed salad and swal-lowed. "It's rather a complicated story and I suggest to you now that we leave it untold."

I said, "I think you know me better than that."

"Yes. I do. All right. I'll start at the beginning." He drank water. "I was introduced to Weiss by a man who thought I might be interested in investing in a movie. I wasn't, but Weiss was bragging about his high-stakes poker game—"just among friends" wink wink—and about this young gun from St. Paul named Sam Zandros. So I called Leo Graff for some information about you and got the story of the Zandroses. Mean-while Carl was talking to a man he knew in St. Paul, named Kelly, I think, who runs a regular game and knows you."

I nodded, said, "Uh huh."

"He and Carl were in the military together. So I went to the game at Weiss's to meet you. One of the things I do is set up poker games. And by the end of the evening I knew I wanted to make you an offer. And I did and I didn't get what I wanted. So, raise the ante. I had a—a contact there in St. Paul who talked to *his* contact there who told him that you were about as tough as they come except where Miss Russell is concerned. That you would do anything for her. There was the key."

I said, "How about some names here?"

He drank some water. The food was getting cold on both our plates.

He said, "My contact was introduced to me by Leo Graff. An asso-ciate of his who wanted to work for me. Be my man in St. Paul. And his contact was—"

Brilliant blinding flash. "My brother Paul." My heart was pounding.

"Yes. Paul Zandros recruited Finny Salter and Gordy Terrell to threaten Miss Russell with serious bodily harm unless you agreed to play in games that were set up on my behalf. But Carl—asked some questions and Finny Salter told Carl that he and Terrell were on their way up to Miss Russell's apartment and they got into an argument about how much he was paying Terrell. Finny Salter stabbed Terrell—strictly self-defense, he says. He was standing there with a dead body and a bloody knife and a gun and a pocket full of cocaine when he saw your taxi pull up in front. He ran to the back of the hallway, to a space under the stairs. He was hiding there when you went upstairs and he ran out the front door when you went into the apartment."

Black waved the waiter over and asked for a glass of white wine and I got another bottle of fizzy water.

He said, "My contact told him he didn't do the job so forget the money, but Finny still needed money, when was it, four months later—I'd guess he always needed money—so he recruited his brother Barry and they went and vandalized the apartment. Without telling my contact, believing he'd have to pay them after the fact. And when they were done with that, the two brothers got into an argument about waiting for her—Miss Russell—to come home, and Finny killed Barry."

I poked at some green beans.

He said, "I didn't know about that second foray, or about Barry, only about Terrell."

I said, "When I stumbled over Terrell, I'd just arrived from L.A. It was only chance that I was even in St. Paul. Why did you think that this would be seen by me or anyone as a message to me?"

He looked ever so slightly embarrassed. "It was something of a training exercise for my St. Paul contact."

I said, "He didn't pass."

He said, "No, he didn't. My contact said Salter had strict instructions not to harm Miss Russell, only to use the—threats as a message to you. But I got the impression from my contact later that maybe he hadn't been very emphatic in passing on my instructions. I'm not sure if that part of their instructions would have—held them back. It certainly wasn't going to hold back Salter. I now very much regret the whole incident. It was bad management on my part."

I looked at my plate, feeling fatigue wash over me.

But I shook it off, finished my dinner and played well, and after the game I found a blondie in the bar. Only five hundred bucks and I even walked her to the door.

Then I stood in the window of my twentieth-story hotel room and drank hotel brandy and looked at the lights of Chicago. Was it done?

Was that it for me and Clare? There was physical pain—in the center of my body—it hurt to breathe. Am I dying?

God, no. I have something left to do.

I don't make bargains with God, though sometimes I ask for help or say thanks. But not this time. This was the sort of thing I do without God.

There was one loose end. Who was the man who set it up, the matchmaker? The one Black hadn't named, just called "my contact". The one who found and hired the Salters?

I wanted to talk to Carl Huxley.

And then I had to deal with Paul Zandros.

Monday, April 16

1

Black was staying in the same hotel—in fact, I thought he lived there—and my bet was that Carl did too. I called the desk and asked for Carl Huxley and in less than a minute I was talking to him.

"It's Sam Zandros."

"Mr. Zandros." He sounded about as sleepy as I figured he ever sounded.

"I want to buy you a drink and pump you for information."

He hesitated for maybe three seconds. "I'll meet you in the bar downstairs. Ten minutes."

I was pretty sure I'd caught him in bed. Yet he showed up dressed, pressed, brushed, combed, and alert within the allotted time.

I had a Hennessy XXO, straight up, in my hand, water side. He ordered a Johnnie Black and water, and we moved to the end of the bar.

I said, "Somebody in St. Paul pointed Finny and Barry Salter and Gordy Terrell at Clare Russell. Based on information from Paul Zandros. Black calls the somebody 'my contact' and doesn't name him. I want to know who he is. I'm thinking you know his name."

He drank and ran his tongue over his teeth. He said, "Going hunting?"

"A little message in deterrence to deliver."

He drank again. "Shooting someone is not like beating up a frat boy in a bar."

"Your boss's research is thorough," I said.

"Yeah." He finished off his drink and waved the bartender over. Definitely off duty. "This guy is not some punk that they're going to sweep to the side. They being the cops. And if you just beat him up, he'll rat you out for sure."

The bartender came and we ordered two more.

"So I walk away?" My tone said in your dreams.

"I'm going to suggest you leave it to a professional."

I said, "That's better?" This time it was a real question.

"It's better than leaving Miss Russell to wait for you outside the Graybar Hotel. You can have an alibi."

"Yeah. But I don't think I know any professionals. Not well enough to ask that."

"Well, you know one." He smiled a very small one-sided smile. Wow. Carl smiles.

"How does the deterrence come in?"

"He has an older brother. The brother gets a message. If he—or any-one—even thinks of touching Miss Russell or anyone in your family— you get the idea."

I said, "Always go with the classics."

He said, "Actually that message was already sent, but maybe to a different zip code. This will reinforce it."

"You have anything personal going on here?"

He shrugged. "I like Miss Russell."

"Do you now."

"And Mr. Black was—dealt a bad hand. From the bottom."

"You seem like a man who's got some ideas about loyalty. Honor, even."

"Marines," he said.

"Yeah. We learned about honor in the family. Mostly it came down to how to be a man." I waved a couple of twenties at the bartender and he brought a check. I could have put it on my room tab but this one I paid, not Hugh Black. Carl watched.

I said, "Does this conversation fit into whatever your definitions of loyalty to Black encompass?"

"Giving you information that he withheld? It's one of the times I get to use my own judgment. I don't see it as being potentially harmful to him. I have my own ideas about why he kept the name back. I believe he wants to protect Miss Russell."

"And my using that information might endanger her?"

"Possibly."

I said, "What I'm proposing is certainly something a man does. But does a man send a proxy to do it?"

"That's what the military is all about. Always has been. Sending someone else." There was an edge to his tone. "That aside, it's a subject I've given some thought to, having been sent in a variety of situations. In the Corps we talk about having a mission to take bullets for the civilians. That's our job. It's also our job to protect by destroying the enemy. I think you're good at a lot of things but you're a civilian."

Oddly, that stung a bit.

He said, "This is just another war. Another battle, another enemy."

The bartender brought my change and I added a ten and pushed it back across the bar.

I said, "Just so we're clear, tell me his name."

"Bobby Graff."

We walked out into the lobby. He said, "Let's step outside."

We did and went across the hotel driveway and stood in a mini park they had made there. It was about the size of a king-size bed, but it had a tree, three bushes, and three kinds of flowers, and a gravel path with a few artistically placed lights, and a large ceramic urn filled with sand. I took out my case of little cigars and offered and he accepted and we stood there and smoked for a minute. No wind off the lake for once. Almost balmy.

I said, "Bobby Graff plays some poker, so I know him a little. New Year's Eve, Clare and I were both at a party in St. Paul. I say both because we were there separately. I was working the poker room and my brother was running a mini-casino. It wasn't Clare's kind of party at all. Big money and the people who have it. But she'd done portraits of the host's family, so she accepted the invitation. Bobby introduced himself and got her off in a corner and hit on her and wasn't going to take no for an answer. Asshole was for raping her right there. I was about to knock him down when my brother intervened. However, you don't say no to Bobby Graff. He's one of those guys who'll destroy what he can't have. Sending someone into Clare's apartment was, I'm pretty sure, payback for that rejection. Doing it for Black was only the kicker."

"Yeah. I heard a couple of stories about Bobby and women."

"Are you going to tell Black about this?"

He said, "No. Well, maybe. If he needs to know."

"This is why Kevvy Smith thinks Black is moving into St. Paul? Because of what happened at Clare's?"

"Apparently so. And Black backing you."

I asked, "How did Black get in touch with Graff?"

"Graff came to him, made a proposal about being what he called a local lieutenant. He'd been in a couple of Mr. Black's games."

We smoked for a while.

I said, "When Kevvy called me to warn me away from Black, I hadn't done anything but talk to Hugh in a bar in L.A. How did Kevvy know about it?"

"Mr. Black had talked to Leo Graff about you. For background. Give me your phone." I did and he punched in a number and the phone in his pocket trilled. He punched *end* on mine and handed it back. He said, "Clare Russell is a brave woman." He threw his cigar into the urn and mine followed it. "There's a game in St. Paul tomorrow night. Tonight. Monday."

I said, "Yeah. Elmore's. Regular game, Mondays, starts about midnight. Not rich but I play there occasionally."

"They know you?"

"Yeah."

"Play there tonight. If possible, get your cousin or someone to play with you. Be there by twelve, earlier if you can. Stay until six, if you can. If you have to leave before that, call me."

He didn't say anything else.

I said, "That's it?"

"That's it."

"So Tuesday," I said, "you own me."

"And you own me."

We stood there a minute.

I said, "What's all this costing me?"

He said, "On the house."

"Come on."

"Bobby Graff is a pimple—comma, pus-filled." A pause. "His attempt to get in with Mr. Black was also an attempt to get me out of the way. I'd been in St. Paul, doing a courier job for Mr. Black, and Bobby and I had a disagreement. A rather public disagreement. He made certain suggestions about my relationship with Mr. Black."

Another minute.

I said, "They say it's best served up cold."

"Yeah."

We walked back into the hotel.

2

I had dinner again with Harry and Karen. After we ordered, she examined my face and said, "You look tired. Are you sleeping?"

I said, "Sure, I always sleep."

Harry said, "You have circles under your eyes."

I said, "I don't."

Karen said, "You do. And so does Clare."

I said sharply, "Is she all right?"

Harry said, "Gotcha," and Karen said, "No, she's not. She's about as all right as you are."

I said, "New subject. I'm playing at Elmore's later."

Harry said, "Are you inviting me to play cards?"

"I am."

Karen picked up my hand and looked at the palm. "Hands of the devil. Look at that."

Her hand was small and warm and Harry's. I said, "Can we hold hands?"

She said, "Yes."

So we did.

3

Harry and I got to Elmore's about eleven and drank a beer at the bar and watched the end of a West Coast baseball game. After enough of that we drifted into the back room, greeted a half dozen other men, and sat down at the table. Harry wasn't talking much and was giving me a look that said, okay but you better explain this later.

Somebody dealt and I was in it. It always worked that way.

About five Harry said, "What time you want to leave?"

We were both way up, and two other guys gave him disgusted looks. He smiled happily at them.

I said, "Soon. Maybe. Dunno."

He said, "Decisive. I like that."

About half past a guy named Buzzy Ellison came in. He'd played earlier for two or three hours, then left for an hour, now he was back. He sat down and said, "You heard?"

The dealer did his thing.

Harry said, "Is this a riddle?"

Buzzy said, "Guy got shot up outside Loop's. Drive-by. Guy in a car stops, says hey c'mere, guy starts walkin' over, four shots."

I said, "Thank you for the news bulletin. You going to play?"

"Oh, yeah. Check."

Somebody asked who was it got killed.

Buzzy said he didn't know.

Someone said pretty fancy venue for a drive-by.

Someone else said *Ven-yue. Wow.*

I folded. When the hand ended I stood up.

I said, "Cash me out, will you?"

Harry did the same and we walked out to his car and got in and locked the doors. He said, "That the news you were waiting for?"

I said, "Ain't safe to be on the streets anymore," and took my gun out of my holster. We had a lot of cash on us.

I told Andy about it, like I always did, but he was the only one.

TUESDAY, APRIL 17

I called Black. "I don't know what you wanted to plan for this weekend, but I can't play."

"Did you get sick after all?"

"No. It's Easter."

"I didn't know you—never mind. Next week?"

"Sure."

WEDNESDAY, APRIL 18

Andy and I were alone in the office, playing gin, when I got the phone call from Carl.

He said, "The other part of the message is delivered. Saw him myself."

I said, "Good. Did it take?"

"I think so."

"Black know?"

He said, "No. Not yet."

"Well, thanks."

"Semper fi."

I said, "Yeah. All of that."

That was when I told Andy, about Carl and Bobby and Paul. We decided we had to do something about Paul but not until after Easter.

SUNDAY, APRIL 22

I was Greek Orthodox from my cradle but only irregularly a practitioner. This year I fasted on Good Friday and went with Catherine and the children to Divine Liturgy on Easter. There were some sidelong glances from down the pew where the family were all strung out to my left.

Did I pray for anything? No. Did I say thank you? No. Did I say I was sorry? No. I wasn't. What was I doing there? I didn't know.

MONDAY, APRIL 23

1

Philip caught me in a rare moment when he and I were the only ones in the office. Besides Cy.

He said, "I don't like this tension in the family."

Since Paul was nothing but suck, Philip was de facto chief executive of the family, Uncle Nick being head of state. I said, "What tension?"

"Between you and Paul."

"It's just me that's tense. He's too dumb." I sat down and put one foot up on a chair edge and leaned back, folding my arms. "You know, one of these days he's going to cause big trouble for the family."

Philip stared out the window. His favorite worrying place. "Yes, I know."

I said, "You know he cheats."

He turned around. "You know this?"

"You didn't know."

He shook his head. "No, I didn't know. Not for sure. I rarely play with him. He wouldn't cheat with me in the game."

"But you're not surprised."

"No. Not surprised."

I dropped my foot and sat straight. "Damn it, do you know how much money he's cost us?"

"I probably know better than you. How do you know he's cheating?"

"I've seen it. So has Andy. Splashing and shorting the pot. He's too clumsy for any mechanic's tricks. We both covered for him and paid the pot the shortage, but we're only doing that for the family, not for him. And he plays in a lot of games we're not in. Someday soon he'll be caught and we won't be there to protect ourselves. And he won't just say oh sorry my mistake. He'll get all blustery and accuse someone else."

"That's small change. Why is he doing it?"

"Because he thinks he's getting away with something."

"Yeah, that's him."

"And I'm pretty sure he's been doing a signaling cheat. I only saw it once and then they stopped. But Andy saw it, more than once. And that could be more than pocket money."

"Who's his partner?"

"Was. It was Bobby Graff. And Andy says he's holding back money from the family."

"Jesus. What money? He's such a bad player, where's he getting it?" He frowned, then sighed. "Sports. Taking bets outside the business. Using family money. Okay. It's time. Call Andy. I'll call Uncle Nick. Make sure they'll both be here this afternoon. Paul told me he'd be in about four."

I said, "About fucking time. But there's more." And I told him about Paul and Bobby Graff and Gordy Terrell and the Salters.

I said, "Andy knows. And Black and Carl Huxley. And probably Leo Graff. And you and me."

He said, "That will all have to wait. We have to get him out of the business first. What you're saying—that just makes it more imperative that we act now. Today." He went to talk to Cy.

2

We were all there. Except Cy. Uncle Nick was in his big armchair, Philip was in the chair behind his desk and I was at mine, and Andy was sprawled in a chair by the conference table. Paul was sitting across from Philip. He was uneasy. Probably he'd never seen us with those faces before. Minds had been made up.

Philip was quick. "You've been cheating at games and you've been cheating the business. Stealing family money. It's only a matter of time before you do something that ruins us. So you're out. Now. Cy is seeing Tim Christides right now, drawing up the papers. And he's getting new signature cards for all the bank accounts. I don't know the exact figures right now, but you'll be getting about six hundred thousand. Maybe a bit more. Plus you'll have Lillian's building. We'll always see to Young Nicky, you know that, but not through you or Lillian. After today, there's no more money for you, either of you, from this business or from any of us."

Paul's voice was hoarse. "I ain't signing any papers that let you take away what's mine. I worked to build this business same as the rest of you!"

I must have moved because Philip held up a hand to stop me. He said to Paul, "You know that's bullshit. We let you stay on too long here, out of sentiment. And you will sign the papers, or some information is going to find its way to people you don't want to deal with."

I *think* he was bluffing.

Uncle Cy, still in his raincoat, came in the door and handed a folder to Philip, who flipped through the contents and handed it back.

Philip said to Paul, "Go with Cy, please."

Paul looked dazed. Uncle Nick stood up and went to him, took his arm, and lifted. Paul rose to his feet and went with Uncle Cy and Uncle Nick, who closed the door behind them.

Philip said, "We need to protect our reputation as much as we can. As soon as he's out of the building, start passing the word. He'll try to get ahead of us, but if enough people know it from us, he won't be able to. Don't mention Bobby Graff. But I'm telling Cy no more bets from Leo."

Andy said, "Will he go to the DA? Or the cops?"

Philip said, "Cy's paper includes *all* eventualities."

The first one I called was Hugh Black. He said he would get in touch with Philip right away to see how they could help.

Then I called Harry. I told him what happened and asked if he could go to Clare's and stay with her for a while. "Until I get something else set up." He said of course.

I said, "Bless you, my son."

He said, "Karen's with me. That okay?"

"Everybody in town is going to know about this by sunup. Why not her?"

Uncle Nick came back in and called Catherine and Sofia. Philip was busy with the security at Catherine's and Sofia's buildings and arranging with Peter and Mike to pick up kids at schools. Andy was talking to Kori's brother, Ted Junior. Uncle Cy was calling the locksmith and going to the bank with new paperwork. I took my gun from the safe and the holster from the desk drawer and put it on. So did Philip, who also kept his there.

"He's my own damn brother," he said bitterly while he was strapping it on. "And yours."

My anger flared. "Yeah." I said, "and so fucking what?"

He turned away.

I sat and thought about Clare. She was by far the most vulnerable and also the one that Paul was most likely to go for. He would know, or suspect, that it was largely my doing that had put him on the streets. But guys in security company uniforms were not the answer.

Andy punched *end* on his phone and gave me a questioning eyebrows-up.

I told him my worries about Clare and said, "I don't know what to do."

He said, "Ask her."

"Ask her."

"Ask her. Harry's there, right?"

"Or he will be soon."

"He can ask her."

3

I called Harry. He was just parking his car in front of her house.

I said, "I have a request."

"I live but to serve you."

Behind him Karen called out, "Me, too!"

"I want you to explain to Clare what's happened here and ask her—tell her I need to—give her some protection for a few days. Ask her what she'll stand for. Paul's going to think I was behind this and he'll be more than half right. He's very impulsive and not very organized, so he's not going to become a sniper—but he might show up there. He once called her the bitch with the cameras."

"And he's still alive?"

"My mistake. Or he might try to follow her or accost her on the street."

"'Accost', eh."

"I'll send you a dictionary. When's your birthday?"

"I'll get back to you."

"Are you carrying? He might be. He probably is."

"Yes, I am. Plus I have Karen. I can throw her at him and run."

Then I sat and stared out the window. What had Paul done? Betrayed the family big time, embezzled, endangering all our livelihoods, and put Clare in mortal danger. She could have been badly hurt or even killed.

But he hadn't actually killed anyone. Finny had done all that. And Bobby had been the mover and shaker. And Black had played the role of the king who cried out, "Who will rid me of this woman who stands in the way of what I want!"

Except she didn't. She never had, and Black knew it. I and only I said no to him, and when he and his underlings—and they *were* his and he knew it—when they brought her into it, I said yes, quick as a fox.

So what to do about Paul?

4

For two hours I played online poker and solitaire on the computer. I hated solitaire on the computer because I couldn't cheat. I also paced. And played gin with Andy until he cleaned me out of my gin stash. I was too rattled to concentrate.

"No game tonight, I hope," he said.

"I'll be all right."

Philip said sharply, "You don't play if you can't fucking sit still."

Harry called. He said, "She wants to see you."

"She what?"

He enunciated mockingly clearly. "She wants to see you. She wants to see you here, when you can get here."

"I'm there." I closed the phone. "She wants to see me."

Andy said, "I'll drive you."

For most of the drive to Clare's, the only thing I said was, "I'd like to get there alive."

Then, as he turned down her block, Andy said, "Will you call me if you need anything?"

"Okay. Yeah. Sure."

I went up onto her porch and rang her bell. Through the big glass in the door I saw and heard Harry come bounding down the stairs. As he opened the door I heard Andy drive away behind me.

5

Harry and I said, "Hey," and I followed him up the stairs. There was now a big fat bulb in the overhead fixture that even in the daytime lit up the shadowy hall and stairs.

The door was standing open and we went in. Karen was sitting cross-legged on a folded futon on a frame, the new sofa apparently, and Clare was standing in the middle of the room.

My God. She was so beautiful. I felt tears coming up in my eyes and my throat closing. I swallowed hard.

She said, "You rang the bell."

"Yeah." I cleared my throat. "Yeah."

"Want a beer?" Harry asked.

"Sure. How far behind am I?"

Clare said, "One," and Harry laughed and said, "Two."

He brought four bottles of Sierra Nevada while Clare and I just looked at each other. Karen unfolded herself and said to Harry, "Let's go in the bedroom and watch TV. We can neck. It'll be like on a date. That all right, Clare?"

"Oh, sure, fine. Yes."

Harry smiled an evil smile at Karen, and she went into the bedroom and he followed her and shut the door.

Clare said, "Sit down."

I sat on a wooden chair. She sat in her desk chair.

She said, "You never rang the bell before."

I lifted the bottle and said, "New times," and drank.

"Yes."

I said, "Do you need me to explain about Paul?"

"No, I think I understand that part. Harry explained it very nicely."

"Well, anthropology and all. Right up his alley."

"Yes. No, I wanted to—say some things. Maybe ask a couple of questions."

"Go ahead then."

She was sitting very straight, with her hands folded on her lap, looking like the firing squad was expected any minute. "Well, I've been thinking about—you—and wishing I knew what to do. I wanted someone to talk to about you, but there was just Harry and I didn't want to... invade your privacy. I was confused and I didn't have any data."

"Data is my middle name."

"Andy came to see me."

"Did he."

"He said you didn't know he was here."

"Right. I didn't."

The rat bastard.

"He called me a gold-plated bitch. No, a gold-plated *fucking* bitch."

I said, "How helpful."

"Well, it was, sort of, really. I guess it—laid the groundwork. Defined where he stood. He was very nice about it."

"Was he drunk? Were *you* drunk?"

"Maybe he was, a little. And he asked me why I was killing you."

"Always the silver tongue, our Andy."

Suddenly she blushed.

I laughed. "Oh, Christ, he kissed you, didn't he?"

"That—that was later. When he was leaving."

"Go on then."

"He said I love Sam and you're killing him and I said I'm not and he said I know what he did and what he didn't." She took a breath. "And he said you're in the right on that one. That I am. Was. He said you were wrong. You. And he said so is this worth it."

Her pronouns were giving me some trouble but I was still tracking.

"He said—he said is being right worth sticking the knife into him? Why don't you just get out an actual knife and shove it in for real? See the blood for real. Then you'd for sure be right. He said you like that idea?"

She choked a little on that part. That goddamn Andonios was playing on her visual imagination, which was probably too good for comfort. And he'd guessed that.

"He said you were raised together. From babies. You slept in the same crib. You fell down the back stairs together. He said I know him better than he knows him. You. He said you were at the university together and even had a few classes together. He said you're brilliant and you could have had an academic career or whatever you wanted. Well, I knew that. But he said you like to play cards and play the odds and take risks and win. He said you like the action and the bigger the pot, the more you like it."

She stopped and looked at me. I just nodded.

She sighed. "He said all you want in your life is the action and your—your barbarian woman! He called me a barbarian!"

I laughed. "He's Greek, you're not. Hence the epithet."

"Yes. Well, then he—talked about my mother and said I couldn't ever please her because she didn't want me to. And then he said—he said—I have to get this right—he said now you've got a man who loves you like crazy—" She was blushing again. "—who cares about what you do, and will take care of you. And you do need taking care of. Me. I do. He'll let you do what you want to do, let you be who you are, and take care of you. So what the fuck is *wrong* with you, lady?"

I was having a little trouble keeping a straight face.

She said, "So *I* said you knew it was those people who wanted *you* who smashed my cameras and you knew they were after you and you let me think it was my fault, that someone was after me." I opened my mouth and she held up a hand. "Let me talk."

I nodded and drank more beer.

"Andy said that those people were Mr. Black and his minions—no *laughing*!—and that Barry's brother worked for Mr. Black—or some-one did—and Barry was *auditioning* for a part with Mr. Black and he paid Barry and his brother to—to trash my stuff so he can give you a preview of what's in it for me if you don't roll over. And you didn't know. But then there's someone named Smith—" She had a very con-fused and frowny look on her face.

I said, "Kevvy Smith. He's a local guy that we run into once in a while. He tells me that Black, who is based in Chicago, is moving into St. Paul. Maybe he is, I don't know. All in all, I don't know exactly what the hell's going on, but I know it has to do with Black and that Salter is a red herring. And either Black told someone to kill Barry or they got into a fight and Barry lost. I don't know that either. Black says he didn't tell him to do it and I tend to believe him. This is one day after your apartment is reduced to smithereens and three days before your show is opening."

I shook my head. "I made a mistake. I decided not to tell you all this. I didn't want you to know that you were on the X marking the spot because of me. So instead you think *I'm* it because of *you*. Too bad I wasn't a psychology major like Andy. I should have told you what was going on. Andy said so, Catherine said so—everybody said so. But I'm smarter than all of them and I won't tell you before your opening."

I finished my beer and waggled the bottle at Clare.

She said, "No, but you go ahead."

I got another one from the refrigerator and came back into the living room. I said, "But, as it turned out, what you knew or didn't know was irrelevant. Black would have done exactly what he did do. In fact, he'd already done his part. Salter and Finny did smash your stuff and if Salter weren't dead, he would be now."

She gave me a startled look.

I said, "What else? The family?"

She sighed. "Andy said all those lives and mine have crossed and nothing can uncross them."

"He's right."

"He said I need someone to take care of me."

"You do."

"Will you—would you expect me to be something I'm not?"

"What the hell are you talking about?"

"Kinder, küche, and—whatever."

"Oh, for God's sake, Clare. We're not Nazis! I won't deny that I want to own you." Her eyes became rounder and I smiled. "So would any red-blooded male. But I really don't care whether you cook, which maybe Uncle Nick cares about and maybe he doesn't, and I think he doesn't. I just care that you take pictures that tell the truth. Your truth. Did I ever," I demanded, "tell you how to take pictures?"

"No."

"You're scared of family, but the fact is that that's where you'll get to do what you want to do. Like Catherine. She wanted to be a nurse-midwife and she did it. Some of the old men thought she should stay home. But she does what she wants. It's the thing to do in our family, doing what you want. And then everybody else helps you do it. And I really don't give a fuck about what anybody thinks outside the family, except for you. And some days Harry. And Karen. Some days." I took a deep breath.

She said, maybe a bit wistfully, "You said we could live however we want."

"We can. We would. Didn't you believe me?"

"It didn't seem possible."

We were both quiet for a while.

She said, "You're a lot older than I am."

"Twelve years, almost. Is that a problem?"

"I don't know. I never thought so. Probably because you're so immature. Andy says the only problem will be that we'll remember different wars."

I laughed. "The wars I know the most about were fought eight hundred years ago and involved the Byzantine Empire."

She said, "You could tell me about them."

I said, "Yeah. I could do that. What else?"

She looked away from me.

I said, "Let's get this done. I can't—I want this resolved. Is it the women?"

"Yes."

"Stop thinking they matter. They don't. Forget them. I don't care about them." I gave her a long look, and spoke slowly. Slowly for my sake, not hers. "There are certain—gender and cultural differences that may not be—amenable to analysis. We have thesis and antithesis without synthesis. Some things just—are."

"Do you really believe that?"

"Yeah, I do."

"But—"

"What?"

She didn't say anything.

"You're jealous."

"Of course I am. I'm Irish."

I said, "I'm not trying to hurt you, or take anything away from you. It really has nothing to do with you."

"All right."

"All right what?"

"Just—all right everything, I guess." She took a deep breath. "I've decided it's part of what you do—are—so I won't care."

"You've decided."

"Yes. I have."

I heard Karen laugh softly in the bedroom.

I said, "Can we go for a ride? There's a place I want to show you."

"Sure."

I stopped at the bedroom door before we left and knocked. "Don't come in," Harry called out.

"We're leaving," I called back. "Lock the door."

"Keep in touch."

6

I opened the passenger door for her and our heads came close as she got in. "Hi, Clare," I said, softly as I could.

"Hi, Sam." She got in and when I got in behind the wheel, she handed me the keys. "Where are we going?"

"My place."

"You don't have a place."

"Do now."

"Where?"

"My neighborhood."

"You don't have a neighborhood."

"Do now."

7

Lowertown. My new neighborhood. Near downtown, an architectural jumble of long-time operating businesses and warehouses, abandoned old buildings, a few newish buildings, and rehabilitated and remodeled old buildings that housed offices, galleries, bars, boutiques, studios, second-hand stores, and a few retail businesses. We were just three blocks from the office.

I parked on a side street across from a solid-looking six-story brick building with a boarded-up large storefront on the first floor and dirty blank windows above. Three wide, shallow stone steps led up from the sidewalk to the double front door—heavy scarred wood deep between two big bay windows, with plywood-covered glass. At the left-hand end of the frontage, there was another door, standard size.

"What do you think?" I asked.

"About what?"

"About my building."

"Yours?"

We got out, crossed the street, and went to the doorway, crunching over broken glass, and tried to peer through gaps between pieces of plywood.

I tapped one of the plywood panels on one of the heavy front doors. "Unbelievable as it may seem, behind this wood there's intact glass, really heavy glass, with beveled edges."

"Can we go in?" she asked.

"Sure."

I took a big brass key, on a ring with two others, from my pocket and opened the door.

Inside it was dark and dirty and the floor was strewn with broken boards and broken glass and old paper and odd bits of metal and wire.

I said, "I think it was an electrical supply store. And apartments above." I found a light switch. Nothing happened. "But no more electrical supply." I took her hand and we moved carefully through an even darker back room. "Next time I'll bring a flashlight."

Outside the back door there were wooden steps leading to the upper floors. "I'll go first," I said.

One of my keys worked in the back door of the second-floor and we went into a small filthy kitchen and down a long dark hallway to a room over the street, where we stood in the dusty quiet and looked down at her car.

I said, "I'm surprised no one's living here. I mean the ones who don't pay rent. Squatters."

She said, "That label always seems so wild west."

We went back to the staircase and looked at the stairs going up. "Do you want to go any further?" I asked.

"It doesn't look very safe."

"Let's go down."

We went back to stand inside the front door and look again at the big open space that was the first floor.

"What are you going to do with it?" she asked.

"Dunno. Thought you might like to have it, maybe."

She smiled. "I feel like you're a cat offering me a dead mouse."

"Yeah, well... "

"It's a lovely mouse. How did you get a whole building?"

"How do you think? I won it in a poker game. Let's go sit in the car."

8

She said, "I didn't know what to do to change what happened."

"No one changes what's already happened," I said, too roughly.

"Oh, you know what I mean! Damn it, Sam—"

"Sorry. You're right. I do know what you mean."

She said, "You didn't call or anything."

"You shut the door, Clare, it was up to you to open it."

"So here's Clare, opening the door."

"Is it?"

"Yes."

I said, "Look. We can go into the details later, but I'm not here to have you cry on my shoulder, then sober up and tell me to go away again."

"I'm not going to do that."

I said, "I still want what I always wanted. What do you want?"

She cleared her throat. "I want to be with you."

I reached for her shoulder, shook it slightly. "Does this mean getting married?"

"Yes."

"You're sure? This is not just the beer talking?"

"Yes. No." She gave me a puzzled look.

I grinned. "Sorry to confuse you. We'll get married?"

She licked her lips. "Yes, please."

The relief that went through me liquefied every muscle in my body for an instant. If I'd been standing up, I'd have fallen down. "You're so goddamned polite." I leaned over the console and rested my forehead on hers. "Okay, Frances Clare, we'll be married." She closed her eyes. "And make babies?"

"Oh, yes," she said.

"You better remember all this when you're sober."

"I will, I swear. I didn't have *that* much beer."

9

On the way back to her place she said, "Will you keep on playing for Mr. Black?"

I thought for a moment, but only that long. "Yeah, I will. I like the games and I like the money. And it'll be safer for you. I made a bargain and so did he."

"Do you trust him? To keep his end, I mean?"

"Yeah, I do. He will."

10

She said, "Park in back. They've got the street posted for sweeping."

I did. Her back yard was an overgrown patch of grass surrounded by lilac bushes. She liked it. She liked to stand on the landing at the top of her outside back steps and look down into her mini-jungle. As I fitted the car into the half of the yard that was hers, Paul came out of the lilacs holding a gun.

I said, "Get *down*!" and I eased myself out of the car, crouching, putting the door between me and my brother, unholstering my gun where he couldn't see it. At this angle, if he actually hit the door, maybe it would ricochet. Uh huh.

"You bastard!" he yelled at me. "You shit!" He was drunk. He stopped and waved the gun around. "You coulda just been smart and we'd all be in the money but you and Andy—you goddamn selfish bastards —you get the money and I get shit. No money for stupid old Paul."

I glanced at Clare. She was folded as far under the dashboard as she could fit, her arm bent to hide her face. I called out, "Put that goddamn gun away and go home. You did this to yourself."

He started crying. "You say family but *I'm* family and you don't care about me! What am I supposed to tell Lillian?"

"What have you ever told her? Tell her it was your idea. Tell her you quit."

He said, "You got your gun? Pull it out and we see who best shooter."

I said, "I am, you idiot. You know that. Go home."

He lifted his gun to shoulder height and fired wide. I heard the bullet thunk into a tree trunk. I ducked, a useless reflex.

I yelled, "You asshole. Cops are going to be here in five minutes. Go home. We never saw you."

He got a panicky look and stuffed his gun into the pocket of his suit coat and ran down the alley. I watched him go. He ran like a two-legged elephant, like a big fat kid.

I turned to Clare and helped her to extract herself. Her face was pale and set, her lips pressed together.

She said in a shaky voice, "I don't like being shot at."

"Of course you don't."

"Will he come back?"

I said, "No. Come on, we're going in and we're not answering the door."

No one came.

11

I called Philip and Catherine and Andy, and they promised to pass it on to the uncles and do whatever they had to do. None of us thought he'd go on a shooting spree. His attention span wasn't that good.

That night we stood by her bed.

I took off my jacket and she said, "You're carrying a gun. So was Harry."

"Yeah. Sometimes I do. We can talk about it another time."

I unfastened the rig and set holster and gun on the floor by the bed.

"I really *don't* want to be alone anymore," she said.

"You aren't." I was maneuvering her arms out of her shirt. "You won't be."

"I'm sorry."

"Forget it now. I don't want to hear that." I unhooked her bra, dropped it on the floor, and kissed her shoulder where the bra strap had made a shallow indentation.

"Do you forgive me?"

"There's nothing to forgive. You were at least half right. We can forgive each other. Tomorrow. Come on, take your pants off."

I undressed myself, got under the cover with her, and lay next to her, the full length of her body up against me.

"Jesus, Clare, I have missed you," I said.

She was soft and relaxed and responded so sweetly and openly that I remembered her laughing at me in a noisy barroom. I remembered wanting her then and thought about the desolation of the last two months without her and tightened my hold.

I'd drawn the ten on the river to fill the nut flush. God in heaven! Glory and triumph were mine!

Call *that* one, damn it.

Acknowledgements

A large number of friends and relations have read this story, all or part, during the writing of it, and have given me invaluable feedback.

Bruce Rubenstein
Catherine Parker
Gary Lindberg
Ian Graham Leask
Alice Phoenix
Simba Blood
Ian Moore
John Buranen
Dave Garland
Gary Jenneke
Tom Gibbons
Lois Bowers
Mary Shapiro
Dick Shapiro
Lorraine Blake
Seth Phillips
Wendy Bradley

Thank you all.

About the Author

Jeane Moore writes books about families that are unusual, gamblers, cops, vigilantes, mercenaries, soldiers, crime, love that grows and love that doesn't, death, murder, friends, and friendship. She has written screenplays, won two major screenwriting fellowships, and had a workshop production. She is a long-time member of the Tornado Alley Writing Group, and an experienced earth-sciences writer and editor.